DEAD IN *THAT* BEACH HOUSE

The Senior Sleuths (Book 3):
Dick and Dora Zimmerman...With Zero...The Bookie

DEAD IN *THAT* BEACH HOUSE

The Senior Sleuths (Book 3):
Dick and Dora Zimmerman...With Zero...The Bookie

by M. Glenda Rosen

[signature]

LEVEL
BEST BOOKS

First published by Level Best Books 2020

First edition

ISBN: 978-1-947915-88-6

This book was professionally typeset on Reedsy.
Find out more at reedsy.com

This book is dedicated to seniors. Appreciate what you've accomplished, all you may even have survived, and enjoy the best you might now have in your life.
And never, ever, let anyone abuse you.

Contents

Praise for Senior Sleuths Books

"I found myself laughing and biting my nails at the same time. Sure, her characters Dick and Dora Zimmerman are no spring chickens, but they're every bit as feisty and resourceful as her younger detectives in her *Dying to be Beautiful* series. The mayhem begins when the "Zimms," along with their cohorts—Zero the bookie, Bertie the flirt and a host of others— find a stranger with a knife plunged in his chest in apartment 506 of their upscale Manhattan condo complex. They're determined to solve this murder mystery as well as other mindboggling crimes they run into along the way. What a ride!"—Author, Claudia Riess, The Art History Mysteries

"This series is the senior version of Nick and Nora Charles, with a humorous touch, a splash of noir, cracker-jack sleuthing, unusual, captivating characters, and fascinating mysteries.*What a hoot. What could go wrong? Plenty, and it's great fun.*" —Marilyn Meredith, Author of The Deputy Temple Crabtree Mysteries.

In *Dead In Seat 4-A,* Dora finds a dead man on the plane across from her. Dick hopes the dead body will go away. The Las Vegas Sheriff wishes Dick and Dora would go away. Along the way our Senior Sleuths and their buddy Zero the Bookie meet cheats, embezzlers and cold-blooded murderers.

Introduction

I recently read an observation about the author Colwyn Edward Vulliamy (1886-1971). "He found it easier to come up with intriguing and unusual narrative premises than to sustain and resolve a complicated plot over the full length of a novel" according to Julian Symons who did a pioneering study of the murder genre.

All this was noted in the Introduction by Martin Edwards in the book *Family Matters* under Vulliamy's pen name Anthony Rolls.

I am grateful for discovering other writers, past and present, with the same disposition as I have for finding a voice in truth through fiction.

There are topics I often feel compelled to explore as I have in this Senior Sleuths Book 3.

Senior strengths, their ability to have passion and love and the unconscionable issue of elder abuse found a voice on the pages of this book.

I believe many seniors can have "A Bold Third Act" by starting something new even as they grow older.

Marcia

Dead In That Beach House

The windows had been sealed shut in a house unused for nearly a century on land worth a fortune now. The two youths figured out a way to break in. Stoned and laughing, within moments they were stunned into fear.

A century old skeleton sat on a dark blue velvet dining room chair.

Two other bodies would be found by the police in one of the upstairs bedrooms.

How many more dead bodies would *THAT* Beach House reveal?

Prologue: The Zimmermans

Zero's girlfriend, Cloud, and I were kidnapped.

We were tied, blindfolded and taken to the basement of The Mob Museum in Las Vegas. Of course, we escaped while the confused kidnappers tried to figure out what to do with us. The police knew what to do with them.

I'm Dora Zimmerman. My charming husband Dick and I are retired, well sort of. We have a condo in Manhattan and another in Las Vegas. We've been called Senior Sleuths but police chiefs and sheriffs are less than thrilled with our sleuthing. They've suggested a couple other names for us. We can't help ourselves, murder seems to find us, or even fall into our laps. Literally.

Our friend and sleuthing buddy, Zero the Bookie, usually joins in our adventures. To be fair he usually has no choice, we drag him along with us although it doesn't seem to take much effort. In Vegas, Cloud, a delightful, Native American woman with her own secrets who Zero met on an online gambling site unwittingly became part of our adventure. It turns out she works for the Bureau of Indian Affairs.

Presently, they seem to be enjoying an affair of their own.

We have other interesting friends and associates, like Frankie Socks in New York who was once in the Witness Protection Program. He keeps an eye on us. He also has connections we feel best not to know about. In Vegas we are often aided by Buzz, who we met years earlier through one of Zero's gambling cronies. Best not to ask too much about him either.

Dick and I have been married for 40 years. He used to be a criminal defense attorney. He defended a lot of good guys. But he defended some bad guys too.

I was a lawyer, then a judge in divorce court. I've said this before: there were some criminals there worse than murderers.

Dick and I see our two grown sons a few times a year. They love us. Mostly from a distance since they think we get into too much trouble.

It changed when we recently got a call from our younger son Jake. His girlfriend Lily's aunt and uncle inherited a 100 year old home in the Hamptons, on the eastern shore of Long Island that's now worth a great deal of money.

The Hamptons became posh and pretentious thanks to big money and big egos. There, amongst the rich and famous and wannabes, we found ourselves involved in more than one mystery and murder. Of course!

Jake asked if we could please come and help. "Lily's aunt and uncle were found murdered."

More dead bodies. Some retirement! I'm doing my best to keep you up to date on our escapades.

I told you about *Dead In Bed*. It was pretty exciting, except for when the bad guys tried to kill us. It's always something, right?

The second time *Dead in Seat 4-A* had us involved in a couple more murders and being chased around The Mob Museum by what looked like the Three Stooges.

I thought it all rather funny.

Dick, not so much.

In the Hamptons, where the land and ocean and sky are beautiful, we encountered plenty of ugly secrets, excessive greed, deceit, revenge and dead bodies.

Well, nothing is perfect!

It has also become a place where far too many of the elderly have been frightened and tricked into selling their homes. Now it seems a few have even been murdered.

Money and greed are the motivations, but read on, my dear friend. Hopefully this all won't shock you too much.

One of Lily's long dead relatives was very interested in witches, witchcraft and even poisons. You can only imagine where this has all led us to.

Miss you.

Love, Dora

By the way, as always, you know I do love Dick to death.

Chapter One
Jake (Jacob) Zimmerman

"I'm calling my parents."

Jake looked out the window at the ocean swells, part of a storm heading east.

"Why?" asked Lily, Jake's girlfriend and business partner.

"They're sort of known for helping to solve murders."

"Sort of? What are they, detectives?"

"Not exactly."

"Okay, what exactly?"

Lily sat quietly, listening to Jake.

"They seem to have an uncanny ability to help solve crimes, especially murders."

"I'm assuming you think they really can find out what happened to my aunt and uncle?"

"Well, yeah, I do."

Lily didn't know any more about Jake's family or their friends. Jake wasn't sure he did either, only he knew Zero the Bookie was like an uncle to him. He met some of their other friends at his parents' fortieth wedding anniversary party a few years back. Now, there was a strange mix of people. Some from when they worked, and some from organizations they had belonged to and supported.

"My folks have interesting friends who help them from time to time. I don't know much more. I've been told it's best I don't know. I agree."

There was the charming Zimmerman smile, just like his father and his grandfather, Jacob Zimmerman, who he was named after had. Jake was good looking, tall, lean and to be truthful, more like his mother, with a sense of adventure and determined curiosity to dig deep into a problem or mystery.

Jake and Lily had been a couple for over six years, still, they kept their own apartments. Lily knew Jake did not have marriage on his mind.

Not at all. Well, not yet anyhow.

Strange how a lot of loving relationships languish with those dreams never fulfilled.

The murder of Lily's aunt and uncle would bring to light her strange, even bizarre family story. One she had not told Jake. Or wanted him to know.

Some family stories should be left behind a cloud of secrecy, keeping out intruders. With Lily's aunt and uncle murdered no one but she now knew the family history.

There are life and death stories in all families.

But death by natural causes or murder?

Chapter Two
Two Stoned Youths...
...and One Old House

Years of ocean mist blowing onto shore and hurricanes slamming the oceanfront house had weakened the wood covering on one of the basement windows. Two local teenage boys, stoned and skipping school, decided it was their mission in life to get inside the old, sealed up house.

"We'll need to come back with a crowbar; bet we can split the wood apart so we can break the basement window and climb inside."

The younger boy nodded then followed the older and equally idiotic boy to a pickup truck they had "borrowed" from his father's landscaping business.

He had heard his father talk about the old beach house, complaining to his wife, "It's an eyesore. It needs some real care and the outside should be painted. The ocean has made a mess of it. The only way to contact the owners is through a law firm here who absolutely won't give out any information. So, there it stands, looking like an abandoned, haunted house."

What bored, stoned, teenage boy wouldn't be tempted to explore an old, abandoned house. Especially when told to "stay away from it."

His father had made it abundantly clear numerous times.

"You get into the house and you'll be asking for trouble."

They certainly found it.

The house had been built in 1919. One year later, in 1920, the owners disappeared without word to anyone. A year earlier they had written a will which included leaving the house in a trust with very specific instructions.

Following those instructions, the attorneys created a trust for the Hamptons oceanfront beach house. Ninety-nine years from the date of the trust, the firm or their successors were to notify living relatives, informing them of being heirs to the property. Until such time the house was not to be opened for anyone or put up for sale.

This meant the beneficiaries of the trust had to accept what was known as "Dead Hand Control." The official legal description being "This is conditioning a bequest to a beneficiary, such that they will only receive the gift if they abide by the conditions of the gift described in the trust."

The attorneys were responsible for monitoring the trust. Over the years some prospective heirs considered it all "legal mumbo-jumbo," although often they used stronger language as they attempted to break the trust and take ownership of the property growing in value year after year.

Lily's aunt and uncle, Alice and William (Willie) Sinclair were two of four people who were contacted by Jonathan Gibson of the Hampton Law Firm, Gibbons & Corbett at the end of ninety-nine years. Two others had passed away a few years earlier.

With her father, Peter Sinclair, Lily had visited her aunt and uncle often in her youth. He too had passed away. She always felt he was far too young but grateful for her aunt and uncle. They were her family.

But Lily had discovered many secrets on their farm in Ames, Iowa. Now they were about to be exposed. She had kept the secret for more than a dozen years since she first snuck inside the locked barn and made the shocking discovery.

She thought about the locked barn and what was inside after her aunt and uncle called her.

"We received a letter advising us of a trust for a house and requesting we go to the Hamptons to meet with the law firm representing it." Willie Sinclair called Lily asking if she would meet them there.

"We need help to understand the details of everything since we know little about big city law and lawyers."

Jake agreed to go with Lily. They could take their work with them. Technology had changed the way many people worked. Plus, he had fond memories of his youth in the beautiful beach community. Although it didn't include murder. Not that he knew of anyway.

However, he did recall, there were plenty of arguments over beachfront properties, new construction, traffic, plovers nesting and noisy summer parties. These gave the rich plenty to complain about.

And complain they did. They sued, they threatened, they wrote letters to the editor and the sued some more. The year-round residents shook their heads in disbelief, trying to ignore them as much as possible.

No one would really be able to ignore what was about to be exposed.

The boys' break-in and discovery began on a spring day. They returned to the century-old house with a crowbar. The sun had set and they got to the window, still stoned, slapping each other on the back, thinking how clever they were.

"Hurry up, it's getting colder. I'll pull one end of the wood while you pull at the other side."

"Quiet, I hear a siren."

The older boy leading the stupid adventure shouted, "It's not for us, no one knows we're here."

"We could get in big trouble."

"Then hurry up, dude. We might find some valuable stuff in there."

With that the board fell away from the window and the crowbar was then used to break the glass, making room for them to climb into the basement of the house.

"Got your flashlight?"

"Sure, it's damn freezing in here and smells awful."

"Yeah, let's find a way to get upstairs."

The younger boy grabbed his friend's arm. "Over there. Let's get out of this basement."

Climbing aged, creaky stairs, they opened the door at the top and walked into a kitchen pantry frozen in time. Cobwebs linked across the cabinets, mouse droppings were everywhere, and the smell was even worse than in the basement.

The older boy pushed opened a door leading first into the kitchen, then another into the dining room where there was a long table with a candelabra set in the middle and twelve dark blue moldy velvet chairs.

"Looks like something from a horror film," joked the younger boy, who suddenly jumped and shouted, "a mouse almost climbed up my leg. Hurry up, see what else is here."

Beginning to feel frightened, the smell getting worse with each step, they found themselves in a fancy sitting room with heavy velvet drapes, two blue matching armchairs and a sofa, where spiders had spun their webs across the furniture, lamps and tables. The boys searched the room with their flashlights and, again everything seemed frozen in time.

They walked closer to two of the velvet chairs in a corner of the sitting room, connected to the dining area. There were large bookshelves with century old books, their lights searching the room until the younger boy screamed, a deathly sound in a house supposedly void of life, where they discovered death.

Shaking and pointing. "There's a skeleton in one of the chairs."

The house smelled of its decay and death.

And, they had not even taken the old stairs to the upstairs bedrooms where two more dead bodies inside the house would later be discovered by the police.

Answers about the deaths would come only after strange turns on bizarre roads of investigation in the Hamptons and on a farm in Iowa.

Secrets were hidden in each place.

The boys rushed back down to the basement and climbed out the window which for now was still the only way in or out of the beach house.

"Maybe we'll even be heroes for finding the body," whispered the younger boy.

"Are you nuts?" The older boy pulled him through the window and both ran back to the truck. "We better get rid of the weed before we call the police."

"Good thought."

Two hours later, Hampton Police Chief Arthur Saunders, a couple of his deputies, the coroner and a forensics team were at the house. They called Jonathan Gibbon to meet them there. "Bring keys to open this damn house. Someone found a dead body in there. I'll explain more when you get here."

Jonathan had often been quoted in the local papers saying, "The house is in a trust. Sorry, I'm not allowed any further comment."

Stories about THAT 100 year-old beach house had been news for years. With the 100 years upon them and dead bodies found in the house, all that was about to change.

Saunders had been police chief on this stretch of the east end of Long Island for over twenty-five years. He was totally bald, over six feet tall with one blue eye and one brown eye. He had scared many a kid straight and convinced more than a few drunks and crooks to mend their ways.

Neither shy nor arrogant, he began the job at the dawn of the land in this area growing in enormous value, with the rich looking to get richer. He had seen the landscape change with one mansion larger than the next rising along the seashore. He had also had no problem speaking his mind. "Shame what's happening, destroying so much beauty for ego and money."

Back at the house, crime scene tape was up, the coroners waiting for the bodies to be put in their van. The local media was taking photos and asking the police chief questions he had few answers for.

Answers would come later. Not easily or quickly.

***

Jake and Lily had checked into a suite at an Inn facing the ocean. She was wondering why she couldn't reach her aunt and uncle. They knew she and Jake were coming and knew where they were staying. Jonathan Gibbon had been told to expect them.

The knock on their door changed all that.

And much more.

"Are you Lily Spencer?"

"Why?" Lily, clearly a cautious city girl.

"I'm Chief Saunders, the Hamptons police. The attorney for the beach house told us your aunt and uncle were supposed to meet you here."

"Yes?" Lily nodded not sure what was happening.

"Your aunt and uncle have been found in their van near the beach house."

"What do you mean found?"

"Sorry, miss, I mean found dead. Murdered."

Tact was not his strong suit.

It was right after the sheriff left that Jake decided to call his parents.

***

As for the two boys, they would have to deal with being in trouble for breaking and entering, but would it really matter much after finding a dead body?

Taken to the police station, questioned, and told to appear in court the end of the following week, they would tell their story many times until the police believed them.

They were charged with breaking and entering and each fined $500. Their parents charged them with stupidity and made them work to pay the fine.

No matter, to many of the other kids at school they became local heroes.

The murderers of Alice and Willie Sinclair figured they had no problems. They had nothing to do with the dead bodies inside the house.

Still, there were some connections.

Chapter Three
Dick and Dora

"Did Jake say why Lily's aunt and uncle were in the Hamptons?" Dick asked as he put his head back on the seat, stretched his legs as much as room in the back seat of the car allowed and closed his eyes as more questions danced around his attorney's analytical mind.

"He said they're from a small town somewhere in the middle of Iowa or Nebraska, I can't remember which one. Some lawyer told them they were beneficiaries of a will leaving them a 100-year old beach house. Jake will tell us more when we see them which will be in a few hours." Dora was relaxing too after the flight from Las Vegas.

Frankie Socks was driving the Zimms, as Dick and Dora Zimmerman were often called by close friends, east on the Long Island Expressway from MacArthur Airport. He kept the music low so he could listen to their conversation, prepared to voice his opinion or offer help. If asked.

He would most definitely be asked as trouble escalated and danger became increasingly imminent. Frankie Socks grew up in a family of mobsters and spent years in the Witness Protection Program. For some reason Dick liked the guy and let him know when it was safe to come back home to New York.

Ever since, a grateful Frankie Socks felt it was his mission to keep a protective eye on the Zimms. Turned out it was a good thing he did.

He heard Dora ask her husband, "Do they have any idea how her aunt and uncle were murdered?"

"No."

"Just no?"

"Yes dear, just no.

"Frankie, I know you're smiling, stop it."

"Yes ma'am."

"Don't call me ma'am."

"Leave the driver alone, dear, there's a lot of traffic. He needs to concentrate so we arrive safely."

Dora gave Dick a light punch in the shoulder and turned to look out the window at land once owned by potato and duck farmers, disappearing to greedy land developers and million-dollar homeowners.

The Zimms had spent many a summer vacationing in the Hamptons with their two sons when they were younger. Once the boys were grown and off to college, they spent only a couple weeks in August there, when the heat in Manhattan sent the natives to various ocean beaches. New Yorkers joked, if you needed your therapist in August you're out of luck, they all leave the city. Which implied everyone had a therapist. Many New Yorkers indeed did. It was part of a NYC survival manual for some.

The Hamptons had been a great place to escape. A stretch of land at the end of Long Island, with a shoreline of beautiful beaches, homes built facing sunsets and sunrises over the sand and sea.

There were unfortunately now, bigger homes, bigger money,

11

bigger demands for services and even bigger problems, especially for the police.

Increased traffic added to all the fuss, many seeming in a hurry, driven by a sense of their own importance. At this time of year, early spring, it had not yet risen to the fever pitch of the summer months. The "season" was known for making the sanest of locals go a bit crazy.

Passing dozens of cookie cutter suburban communities spreading further and further east, there were small and large shopping centers and malls, until the road split, dividing the North Fork and the South Fork.

They were very different worlds. The North Fork was home to wineries and a less intense lifestyle. The South Fork, known as the Hamptons, well it seemed there was no end to it being a privileged lifestyle there for many.

The view going east on the South Fork changed to farm stands, restaurants with names like Lobster Inn and the Fish Folly, and less crowded landscapes with the enticing smell of the sea.

"Dick, you or Dora want to stop anywhere first?" Frankie Socks slowed down, waiting for an answer. He was also waiting for answers from messages he'd left for a couple of friends who would be useful in dealing with problems he expected might arise. Smiling and thinking to himself there were frequently problems arising when the Zimms were around.

"Dora, let's stop at the farm stand before we get into town and meet up with Jake and Lily. Makes me feels like we're out of the city."

"Dear, if you look out the window, I believe you'll know you're out of the city. Sure, stop. While you shop, I'll let Jake know we're here and plan a time to meet for dinner."

Dora dialed her cell phone. "Your dad is buying fruit and vegetables at Barney's Farm Stand, wants to feel Hamptonish."

Ignoring the information, Jake told her, "I made a reservation for the four of us at the Beach Grill, seven p.m. Are you sure your friend Frankie won't join us?"

"Oh no, dear, he has plans of his own. I have no idea what and prefer not to."

"See you later."

"Wait, Dad wants to ask you something."

Leaning against the car as Frankie walked around squeezing fruit, Dora stared at him. The whole scene seemed ludicrous to her. Who knows what stories he could tell or what secrets he held from when he was a youngster hanging out with the mob?

Dick finished shopping and took the phone from Dora. "Jake, bring any photos or information Lily might have about her aunt and uncle. Wait, now your mother wants something."

"Dear, ask Lily to check her computer to see if there have been any death notices about her aunt and uncle in their hometown papers. I know it may be too soon, but I'm curious what they would write."

"Will do. And Mom, thanks."

Dick and Dora had a large suite reserved at the same Hampton Beach Resort Inn for themselves plus two smaller suites, one for Frankie Socks and another for Zero. He would arrive by car within a couple days. Zero, as always, refused to fly. Dora wanted to know if he was arriving with or without Cloud.

"I'm not sure if she's coming with me." Zero laughed.

"Sure you are. You just want to keep me guessing."

"Lady D, would I do that to you?"

13

They were both laughing, enjoying the type of banter they shared as good friends since they were in high school together.

Twenty minutes later, Dick was stuffing bags of fruits and vegetables from the farm stand into the small refrigerator in their suite, along with several bottles of wine, a six-pack of beer and some sparkling water they had picked up at a local deli.

Dora unpacked and then read her emails. She was not at all surprised there were none from Zero or Cloud. Dora considered Cloud her friend too, after all they had recently managed to fend off more than a few crazy people in Las Vegas.

Dressed "Hampton Casual," wearing spring jackets as evenings were cool, they walked the few blocks to the Beach Grill. It faced the sand dunes and miles of ocean and provided a view of colorful sunsets, proving murder could and did happen in the best of places.

Lily and Jake walked in holding hands. When Jake saw his parents, they hugged him and Lily. Family. To Dick and Dora Zimmerman, all else paled next to family. Loving them, caring about them, being there for them.

Lily was as Dora remembered. She came up to Jake's shoulders, slender with long dark brown hair and huge green eyes. She was Jake's match intellectually. She was carrying a large deep yellow leather tote bag overflowing with papers that hopefully would explain some of the story about the century-old house and how it had become her aunt and uncle's inheritance.

And now it would belong to Lily. Dora wondered and worried if it meant she was in danger.

"Jake asked me to give all these to you." She was clearly moved by all that was happening. Lily had tears in her eyes. It was such an unexpected and still unexplained loss of her aunt and uncle happening in such a cruel and brutal manner.

Dora put her arms around the slim and pretty young woman who so clearly adored her son. "Dinner now. Tomorrow we'll start looking into what happened to your aunt and uncle."

Dick told them, "Come to our suite around two, we have lots of fruit and drinks." Jake looked at his mother and the two of them raised their eyebrows and tried not to laugh at Dick's announcement. He wisely ignored them.

What a story this turned out to be. It ultimately led them to the original owners and a trail of criminal behavior including more than a fair amount of deceit leading to murder.

Meantime Frankie Socks had taken the car to meet a few old friends at a diner farther east and off the highway. The diner was between two of the Hampton villages, set off to the side, where confidences could be spoken. The old diner had been modernized with mirrors and glass cases near the entrance filled with fancy pastries. There were also special booths in the far back which served his privacy purpose.

Frankie Socks always had a purpose.

Chapter Four
Lily's Aunt and Uncle Sinclair

*A*lice and William (Willie) Sinclair were found murdered in their van, blocks from the house they recently inherited in the Hamptons on Long Island, NY. Married for over 50 years, they were in their early 70's and had lived their entire married life on a farm in Ames, Iowa. They owned a thriving hardware store in town and over the years had grown corn and other crops, some for themselves and some for their neighbors. They were known for being extremely and surprisingly generous.

They had one daughter who died at the age of five from scarlet fever. Their grief sat with them the rest of their lives. Willie survived a stroke two years after she died and walked with a limp and cane for the rest of his life. This paper and community mourn its loss. We expect to share more news with you as we get it.

Dora read the brief write up in the local Ames, Iowa paper and asked Lily for more details about her family.

"My father Peter Sinclair was three years younger than Willie. He brought me to visit my aunt and uncle a few times a year. We filled a void for each other. My mother died in childbirth, providing enough grief and plenty of love to go around. My father and I lived a bigger life in San Francisco. He was an architect and I grew up around culture, money and interesting people, but I loved those visits to Ames, Iowa, and remember them with great affection."

Dora could instinctively sense Lily was intentionally leaving out pieces of the story.

Lily knew she was too, especially why she had been told by her aunt and uncle to never go into the locked barn. She also never talked to her father about it.

For now, deadly questions hung in the air. Perhaps some of the papers they found would reveal how Willie and Alice could afford to often be so generous to Lily as she was growing up.

The farmhouse was located ten miles out of town and daily, except Sundays, Willie Spencer went to work at the hardware store. Alice joined him Friday and Saturdays, their busiest days, and other days too as he aged.

They hired additional help for the store over the holiday seasons. They continued to go to church functions, to donate to local charity events and send truly generous gifts to Lily for her birthdays, holidays and any special occasion.

Lily would call and chastise them for being too extravagant and they would laugh.

One day her uncle called to tell her, "We're sending you a key and information about our safe deposit box. You need to sign the card and send it back. We want you to be able to get to our papers. Well you know, when the time comes and we're no longer here."

Two huge dogs guarded the farmland property. Ames neighbors joked about it. "Someone going to steal stalks of their corn? Maybe take one of those delicious pies Alice makes every year for the county fair? Who knows, could be they're hiding something." Ames gossip kept at it year after year. If only they really knew!

Lily was now the sole beneficiary of their will, which included the house and land in Ames and the trust for *THAT* Beach House in the Hamptons. She knew she would have to tell Jake and his parents what she had discovered in their barn.

She would have to try and explain what she had always thought of as the unexplainable.

Everything was connected, the old and the new.

They were connected by money and murder. By past and present.

Chapter Five
Murders In THAT Beach House

One hundred years had passed between the murders of Lily's aunt and uncle and those decaying bodies locked in the house, thanks to the restriction imposed by the trust.

Police Chief Arthur Sanders allowed Lily, Jake and his parents to visit the beach house, in hopes they might be able to shed some light on what had happened.

Before the visit, Dick and Dora read through the papers Lily had requested from the law firm handling the trust.

Lily, Jake and his parents moved slowly through the house, the reality of death heavy as they walked from room to room. The cobwebs, thick layers of dust and mice droppings would be cleaned and cleared later when the yellow crime scene tape was removed.

"Why would anyone want to kill them? They've never even been to the Hamptons." Lily obviously and understandably was having difficulty processing what was happening.

She stayed downstairs with Dick while Dora and Jake went upstairs. They wandered in and out of the bedrooms and several bathrooms. The police had already left their footprints in the dirt and dust smothering the floors.

Dora opened closets and dresser drawers, moved around old fashioned clothes and felt something hard under a long black and white striped petticoat.

"Shh, come with me." Jake knew that shh meant: "Don't tell Dad." They had that secret code since he was a young boy.

***

For over a century the Hamptons had been a magnet for artists and writers. The views, the sea, the sunsets drew them into Nature's web. But the Sunset Development Group didn't care about any of that. They were aggressively attempting to buy up numerous parcels of prime land facing those views.

For years **THAT** Beach House they wanted stood alone on slightly over an acre of land, isolated behind sand dunes where it had been built for a fraction of the cost of what it was worth today.

For the last dozen years the law firm of Gibbons & Corbett kept telling them, "No, it is not possible to buy it until the 99 years is up as stated in the owners trust and will."

The original owners had left the law firm a substantial amount of money for yearly taxes and minimal upkeep on the outside of the property, but it was clearly decaying inside.

It really didn't matter if the house rotted and was reduced to rubble. It was the land that was worth a fortune to developers.

***

The house had originally been built by Lily's great-great uncle, James Sinclair.

"I never met him. My uncle Willie said he was not a very nice man. I never knew what they meant by that."

It would be discovered that one of the decaying bodies found was his wife. The other two skeletons, two females, were found by the police in an upstairs bedroom on top of a tattered beige lace bed cover. They were his wife's sisters.

All three 100-year old murder victims were proven through the coroner's examination to have been strangled to death after first being poisoned. Aunt Alice and Uncle Willie Sinclair had a better chance of receiving justice for their murders.

Not that being shot in the head at close range was any less despicable.

***

Sewn inside the striped petticoat were two old metal skeleton keys.

Dora and keys. They did get her into trouble.

Jake took pictures of the keys with his cellphone and he and his mother agreed it would be best to show them to Dick and Lily. Then they would forward the photos of the keys to the sheriff, and explain where they were found.

Lily and Dick had found their own surprise in the library. There were several shelves of books about murder. Another shelf had books on witches, witchcraft and poisons. All the dust and cobwebs on them couldn't hide the strangeness of it all.

Dora was determined to come back as soon as possible to look deeper amongst the pages of murder and evil. It only made sense the books might reveal some truths about the house and its owner.

The dust that was unable to hide strange markings on those

21

books made Dora very curious and determined to look for possible answers inside their pages.

"What kind of people owned this house?" Jake looked at his mother, clearly wanting to get out of there.

Chapter Six
Prime Land

"We'd like to speak to Lily Sinclair."

Dora had opened the door to two men dressed in Hamptons business clothes. Meaning shirt, sports jacket, no ties, jeans, and loafers without socks. They announced they were from the Sunset Development Group. As individuals they didn't matter, as a group they were powerful and determined.

Dora's antenna went into full alert as they gave fake smiles and, attempted to get into the suite of rooms where she and Dick were staying. "It's very important. We were told we might find her here, ma'am."

Oh, oh, there it was, ma'am again. Clearly assuming Dora was a sweet lady who was blocking the way to their big dreams for more big money.

"Well maybe I could be of help?" She was dripping with coyness.

"Oh, I doubt it ma'am. We want to help her settle the beach property. Surely it's been such a terrible situation for her."

The older and shorter of the two men, with a full head of grey hair and dark brown eyes, took Dora's hand as if to show how much he wanted to be of help.

Pulling her hand away, she said, "Oh my, you're all too kind, so sweet of you."

Dick heard her replies and practically fell on the floor laughing. He knew her pretense voice. *Now what* he wondered.

"Darling, can you come here? These lovely people want to help Lily."

Dick was delighted to play along. It was not the first time someone tried to sweet talk them and not the first time they played along.

He walked to the door with a limp and slightly bent over. Dora could hardly contain herself. She turned away before they saw the big grin on her face.

"If you could let us in to wait for her, we could make the arrangements rather quickly. We have these papers for her to sign so she could just get rid of that mess and be able to leave here.

"Sweetheart, these people want to help Lily get rid of that ugly old house. Doesn't that sound wonderful?"

The two men from the Sunset Development Group were practically salivating while still trying to push the door open more so they could enter the suite.

"Why, I can't get over how kind people are here." Dora smiled so sweetly.

Having distracted them, Dora grabbed the papers they were holding and handed them to Dick. Then looked up at them with that same smile they would soon come to dread.

"By the way this is my husband, Dick Zimmerman."

No longer limping or bent over, he reached out to shake their hands. "He's a retired attorney. I'm Dora Zimmerman, a retired judge. Once we look these papers over, we'll show them to the sheriff and to the lawyers for the property."

Dick added, "Don't feel left out, we'll be inviting you to those meetings."

The two men stormed off as the Zimms slammed the door after them.

After reading the offer and contract, Dick laughed and commented to his wife of forty years, "Darling, I do think perhaps they were not being very honest."

It was a huge understatement.

It was also a huge miscalculation on the part of the Sunset Development Group and one they would seriously regret.

First, there would be many more twists and turns related to THAT Beach House than anyone could have imagined.

Chapter Seven
Frankie Socks and Friends

The last booth next to a darkened window facing the alley behind the diner always had a reserved sign on it. Locals new better than to attempt to sit there or anywhere near it. The pretense being it was for the owners. The truth was it was reserved for a quiet group of friends of the owners.

He had been one of them in his younger days. For now, he was content to provide his old friends with a safe place to meet.

They were waiting there for Frankie. His arrival brought together long-ago friends who had shared time with him in the mob. There were a couple of hugs, several pats on the back, and silent grins from the four men and one woman as Frankie sat in a chair, they had pulled up to the end of the brown leather booth.

It was his meeting. He requested it through the owner.

A waitress was waved away.

"Murders," Frankie announced.

He told them what he knew from listening to Dick and Dora in the car on the ride to the Hamptons. They understood the way the old days had taught them, and he added, "My boss and his lady," as he called them, "are surely going to need help."

One man simply replied, "Ok. What?"

"For now, whatever information you can discreetly find out about *THAT* Beach House. Who are the people trying to buy it, anything you can find out about the attorneys for the house and if anyone might be bragging they killed an elderly couple in their van."

They memorized his cell number to text information as they got it. Then, Frankie waved the waitress over, food and drinks were ordered, talk turned to politics, the weather and how nothing tasted as good as the pasta dishes in Little Italy restaurants.

Two hours later, Frankie Socks waved goodbye. "See you back here tomorrow, same time."

Chapter Eight
The Keys

They looked the same.

Two large metal skeleton keys from the early 1900s. Each one opened a separate lock.

But where?

Standing outside, walking to their cars, the house looming behind them, dark clouds hovering as if a warning of what was hidden, what had not yet been explained.

Later, Frankie Socks who had driven Dick and Dora to the house watched them walking quietly to the car. Lily and Jake's rental Jeep parked behind him.

Almost all young people in the Hamptons either drove a Jeep or sports car. Image mattered. Money mattered. One couldn't help wonder if murder mattered in this place where beauty and greed collided.

The photos of the keys would add another focus to the investigation.

Lily gasped as Jake showed the photos on his phone to his father and Lily.

"Where did you get them? Why do you have them?" Lily was obviously shocked.

"We found them sewn into a petticoat in one of the upstairs bedrooms," Jake told her.

Dick put his arm around Lily. "Do you know what they're for?"

"Please, I need to sit down."

Frankie rushed to open the Jeep door for her. She slid in, her face pale. If it had been possible, they would have seen her heart pounding.

She sat back, and slowly began to explain. "One opens the barn at my aunt and uncle's farmhouse."

"The other key?" Dora asked.

"I'll tell you. Later. I promise."

With that Jake forwarded the photos to the sheriff explaining where they were found. He did not mention Lily's knowledge of them.

The keys had surely been involved in the century old murders.

And much more.

Chapter Nine
The Trust, Will and Crimes

James Sinclair, Lily's great, great uncle hired an architect and building contractor once he purchased the exact parcel of land in the Hamptons he wanted. His research brought him to the property, desolate at the time, along the eastern coastline. He decided it was perfect for his plans.

He brought his wife to live there along with her two older, spinster sisters. It was furnished and decorated with great care. Soon after it was completed, he murdered all three of them.

He secured the law firm of Emmett and Gibbons after interviewing several, had them write an iron-clad trust and will. He paid them well, very well. He had a lot of money no one knew about. Not even his wife.

He gave the money required for anticipated ongoing services for the houses both in the Hamptons and for the farm in Ames. He provided the names and addresses of his surviving family.

The firm kept a copy and he put one in a safe deposit box along with keys to the house to be given to those in the generation who would be alive in 100 years. The firm was also responsible for communicating with the heirs once a year so they could be made aware of who was still alive. And who was not, until the house was ready to be opened.

James Sinclair was methodical in his actions and demands. They were also diabolical.

After signing the papers in 1920, he locked and boarded up the house, leaving the dead bodies. No one heard anything of him again until a death notice appeared in a San Francisco paper.

"James Sinclair, age 78, was killed in a hit-and-run accident. If anyone has information, please contact the police."

No one ever did.

His life was a complex series of lies, deceit, criminal behavior and more than one murder. He believed his mother was a witch who tormented him until he ultimately released her from his life.

She was his first murder.

He had often asked her, "You're cruel and evil, why did you ever have a child?"

"Oh, darling, be grateful I saved *you*, not like the others."

The first time he heard her make such remarks, his father had died weeks before he was born, he thought she didn't mean it.

He came to discover she not only meant it, she enjoyed tormenting him.

"Why, you ungrateful child. You too should have been disposed of."

"You're a witch. I wish you were dead."

Versions of those nasty fights went on until he was fourteen years old and she came at him with a knife, screaming and threatening him, "I don't want you to be alive anymore. Die. Die. Die."

He recalled her telling him to die and acting totally crazy.

She was dressed in a flowing black dress running after him

with the knife.

He stopped, suddenly, realizing he had grown big enough and strong enough to turn the murderous attack on her. As she lay dying, she laughed, sounding much like a witch to the young James Sinclair.

He left her there bleeding and dying, walked away, far away and never looked back.

Her hate and evil had penetrated his being forever. Over the years he became obsessed with witchcraft, collecting many books on the subject. Books he brought to the beach house along with dozens on murders and murderers.

***

The Sunset Development Group had unsuccessfully attempted to break the trust for over ten years. They were a group of five, three men and two women, who were unscrupulous, greedy and willing to do almost anything to get properties they wanted on the east end of Long Island.

Two of the men and one of the women were owners of a large real estate company. One of the men was a well-connected politician and another member was a woman trustee from an area synagogue.

The only attribute they shared was greed. Well, and a willingness to do whatever it took to get what they wanted.

They had purchased and sold large parcels of property. Purchased extremely cheap from seniors who needed the money. From seniors whose families had lived there for generations. They were sold to the rich and entitled for outrageously large sums.

The members of the Sunset Development Group were

ruthless in their tactics.

But had they now resorted to murder?

"Who are these people buying and selling our land? They are stealing from the elderly by intimidation and verbal abuse. Has it become physical abuse as well? Perhaps even murder?"

Calvin Osborn, in his late forties and editor of the local paper for nearly fifteen years, frequently ran similar stories. Well respected in the community he easily acknowledged no woman would put up with his long hours. He loved his work.

There were often comments to him in letters to the editor. Unfortunately, the Sunset Development Group had connections and were determined to keep the truths about their activities from being exposed.

Was it possible they were about to overplay their ambitions?

Osborn ran a special editorial ending with *"Who murdered the elderly couple from Ames, Iowa? Was it to gain access to THAT Beach House now worth a great deal of money? The police have said no comment to our requests for information and an interview."*

Meantime, Frankie Socks' friends had discovered plenty.

Chapter Ten
Local Investigation

"What the devil is going on with this investigation? Get those two boys who broke into the beach house back here." Chief Art Saunders was barking orders at one of his two senior deputies.

Deputy Earl G. Taylor, a stickler for using his middle initial, was a man often in need of an attitude adjustment. He knew better than to play his attitude game when the chief was mad. Like now!

"Those boys have been bragging at their school about breaking into the beach house and now traffic up and down Dune Road looks like a raceway for teenagers. They're speeding by, throwing things on the property and shouting curses. They think it's a joke."

"They're just having fun, sir," Taylor commented and shrugged his shoulders as if it was no big deal. Saunders was now furious with him.

"What is wrong with you? There were three people dead in the house and two in the van. You think whoever killed those two won't go after those kids? Get out to the school and bring them back in here with their parents."

Chief Saunders followed Taylor out of the police station. The two of them stopped dead in their tracks. In fact, they were quite speechless as they were asked, "Officers, could you kindly direct me to The Beach Inn?"

In a yellow 1970's Cadillac convertible with the top down, wearing an Indian Headdress and a yellow t-shirt printed with, 'just married' the driver was directed by the police chief no less.

"Continue on Main Street a few blocks, make a right on Beach Road, go over a small bridge and you'll find it. The Inn is right there."

"Mighty kind of you, sir."

Saunders looked in the back of the car and saw a Native American woman asleep wearing the same t-shirt.

He turned and walked away, seeking caffeine and comfort food. He had a feeling he would need it.

How right he was.

The investigation was becoming more and more complicated. He was dealing with 100 year old dead bodies, murders and the family of the recently murdered couple, the media, the real estate developers, troublesome teens and now this. "I should have taken early retirement," he mumbled to himself.

Walking away from the Caddy, Saunders took out his cell phone. "I'm going to need some help."

Off and on over the years Sanders found himself collaborating with people who had spent time in federal prison. He had met these former bad guys through unusual circumstances and connections years before They could find out things that had helped him catch some criminals.

It began with a murder of one of their friends, then there was a bank robbery followed by several men and women who went on a stealing spree targeting Hampton homes shut down for the winter. Everyone agreed how tempting it was. Here were these huge homes, left empty with hundreds of thousands of dollars of valuables inside.

Amazing what one could discover hidden in the dark corners of the wealthy Hampton communities. Many of the people caught seemed on the surface to be honorable, law abiding citizens.

All too often for many it was an illusion.

Saunders contacts were the same people Frankie Socks had known during his own very active criminal life.

There was a shocking truth at the end of this mess.

Chapter Eleven
Zero

Married? Really?

Pulling up in front of The Beach Inn, Zero called Dora and announced, "We've arrived."

A young man, staring and trying not to laugh, was taking their luggage out of the trunk as Dora and Dick came out with Jake and Lily behind them. Zero was in full Indian Headdress and both were wearing their bright yellow t-shirts announcing their marriage with silly grins on their faces. They reached out to hug everyone while Dora, managed to ask, "What is this all about?"

"We're sort of married," Cloud announced as she reached in the back seat for a large hatbox.

"WHAT DOES *SORT-OF* MEAN?" Dick and Dora shouted at the same time.

Zero, putting his arm around Cloud, made an attempt at explaining. "See we were visiting Cloud's family on the reservation in New Mexico. Guess we might have had a lot to drink and smoked a peace pipe. I think. Anyhow I'm told a wedding ceremony was performed. So here we are."

Cloud handed the hatbox to Dick. "Since you couldn't be there to be his best man he brought you this to celebrate later."

Dora grabbed it away, took Cloud's arm, introduced her to

Jake and Lily. Zero gave Jake a big hug. "How's my God-son?"

***

All sorts of hoopla went on until they went inside the Inn.

Someone watching them for the development group was reporting in. "Yes, I tried to put a bug in the phone in their suite but it was impossible with so many people in and out of it. In fact, I think they're all more than a bit crazy and we better be damn careful. The guy who arrived in a bright yellow Cady had on an Indian Headdress, so I do mean hoopla. I'll try to get the bugs in there later.

"Damn it. Do it."

***

Once inside everyone settled down to lunch, drinks and to fill Zero and Cloud in on what had happened and what they should do to help find the killer or killers of Lily's aunt and uncle.

As the afternoon settled down, it seemed quite clear to all of them what needed to be done. Several of them would go to Ames to search for answers at the farm, including checking out the locked barn.

"It has to be me." Lily stood up, surprising them with her determination. "I know the area. I know the farmhouse and I've been in the barn, although no one has known that until now."

Dick and Jake were determined they were who should go with her. Within a couple hours all travel arrangements were made.

Dora, Zero and Cloud would stay behind and go back to

search the beach house for any additional clues. Dora was especially interested in the dozens and dozens of books on the still very dusty shelves and hoping Saunders would agree to let them go in again.

It was after seven p.m. when Jake and Lily went into town to pick up dinner for everyone. No one felt like going out. When they came back loaded with several bags of food from a popular Chinese restaurant, Jake attempted to sound casual. "I'm sure we were being followed."

Dick picked up his cell phone and called Frankie Socks and told him.

"Okay."

He didn't have to say anything more.

Something sinister was definitely going on in this community. Dick knew Frankie and his friends would find out who was following his son Jake. No one took this lightly. Whoever murdered the Sinclairs might well be feeling threatened.

After dinner, Cloud brought the hatbox over to Dick. "For you."

Slowly opening the box, Dick looked inside and rolled his eyes.

"Dick, dear, you now have your very own Indian Headdress."

Dora couldn't stop laughing!

Chapter Twelve
Confidences

The day before leaving for Ames, Frankie Socks called Dick. "It's urgent, I need to see you."

"Okay, but Zero is coming with me."

Zero and Frankie were not the best of friends. In fact, they actually sort of annoyed each other, most likely because each wanted to be more important to Dick and Dora than the other.

There were no initial pleasantries, it was in no way meant to be a social meeting. The conversation started as soon as Dick and Zero sat down with Frankie and his friends. They were in the same back booth and nodded okay as different people in the group spoke, one at a time offering information and advice.

"First, you can't tell the police or media for now."

"You're all being watched and sometimes followed."

"Check your phones at the Inn for bugs."

"Lock up all information you find in a safe at the Inn."

"There's an outfit called the Sunset Development Group and they're buying homes on the cheap by scamming the elderly and then selling them for a huge profit. They're dangerous. Do not trust anyone involved with them including the Gibbons & Corbett Law Firm. Before you say anything, yes, we know Jonathan Gibbons is the lawyer for the beach house."

Dick interrupted, "How many in the group are there?"

"Five," replied Frankie Socks.

"Do you know who killed Lily's aunt and uncle?" Dick looked up at them.

"Not yet." Again Frankie responded to him as the others looked on, deadly serious about their intent to keep helping.

"Are we actually in danger?" Zero asked looking at Frankie Socks.

"Yes."

"Do we need protection?" Dick worried for his family and friends.

"Again, yes. We'll take care of it."

Chapter Thirteen
Beach House Sleuthing

The Iowa contingent left for the airport by seven a.m., Frankie driving them to MacArthur Airport in Islip. The meeting the evening before proved they were all in a great deal of danger. For now, this knowledge required caution, secrecy and paying careful attention to their surroundings. There was some comfort in knowing they would be protected by Frankie Socks and friends.

Dick had one final word of advice, really like a demand: "No one goes anywhere alone. Understood?"

***

Chief Saunders gave Dora permission to search the house another time provided she promised to share any new findings with him. "I expect you to let me know if you discover anything else. But, only me, understand?"

Saunders was playing it safe. He clearly didn't trust too many people at this point of the investigation.

***

Dora was anxious to get back into the beach house to search through the books in the library. Her years as a judge had proven she had terrific instincts. She needed them with the many crazy and sometimes outright cruel people she dealt with for many years.

There were some in particular she found the most appalling. They were the people who abused children or made them pawns in terrible marriages.

Zero drove Dora and Cloud to the beach house in the yellow Caddy, the top up, the weather having turned once again towards dark skies with rain predicted.

In the meantime, the beach house was being watched courtesy of the Sunset Development Group.

The farmhouse and barn in Ames were also being watched.

They were making serious miscalculations about the people who had come to help Lily Sinclair. Still, their ambitions made them often act irrationally.

Chapter Fourteen
The Spencer Farmhouse

The farmhouse, on several acres of land ten miles outside of Ames, Iowa, sat in the middle of what looked like miles of nothing to big city people. It was surrounded by land where the owners grew crops they sold year after year and an area where trees bent over a weather-beaten barn as if wanting to hide it.

There was a fence, the wooden gate now broken, built years ago to keep in horses.

Still, on the surface, everything seemed to appear to be a normal farm in the middle of Iowa.

Nothing was what it seemed.

Lily told them the house had three modest sized bedrooms, a living room, large kitchen, separate pantry and one bathroom. There was a small attic with a window facing the barn and a large basement.

The locked barn would tell its own story.

Dick, Lily and Jake had flown into Des Moines, rented a car, set the GPS north to Ames and then to the farmhouse.

"I used to play in the attic with a friend, the same age as me, we met at a family party when I first visited here. We pretended we were princesses in a castle. All seems so innocent and silly now."

Her friend was no princess. Divorced twice, Charlene Miller had three children, and was struggling to manage a farm her family owned since before she and Lily were born.

Lily called her and after strange hellos, after all, it had been many years since they had spoken or seen each other, said

"I wanted to let you know my aunt and uncle were murdered. We're here to close down the house and sell the property."

Charlene jumped at the chance to contact the one real estate office in Ames. She was hoping there might be some money in it for her especially since she remembered the house she and Lily played in as young girls so long ago.

There had long been rumors about the strange behavior of Lily's aunt and uncle. They seemed to always have much more money than their farm and the hardware store could possibly provide. Much more. Talk had been there must be money hidden somewhere on the property, their two large dogs kept unwanted visitors away.

"I'll call the real estate office and let them know, give me your cell number so they can contact you."

It set in motion more than they could have ever anticipated.

Lily had a key to get into the farmhouse. One she had been given many years earlier. Her aunt and uncle had left the house perfectly neat and tidy.

"I'm sure they thought they would be coming back here. There's food in the freezer and lots of dog food. They always had a lot of dog food." Lily sat down her head in her hands. I forgot, we better make sure the hardware store is closed, maybe the real estate people can also handle sale of it."

They searched the house thoroughly. Every room, closet and drawer were opened and checked for some clue. After they looked a couple of hours, Dick decided he wanted to recheck the pantry area. Something about it didn't fit.

"Jake, Lily, help me take everything off the shelves in this pantry."

"Dad, it's only old canned goods."

"Exactly, anyone who would eat anything in them could be sick or worse. Why keep them if they're so old?"

Jake took one whole shelf of cans and pushed them onto the floor, Dick taking a few at a time placing them on the same floor, raised his eyebrows and grinned at his son.

Jake suddenly stopped tossing the old cans of food on the floor. "Dad, here, the backboard to this lower pantry shelf is loose."

He had pulled out a large, worn canvas bag and set it on the floor between him and his father. Opening it they found hundreds of dollars in cash, legal and financial papers, old newspaper clippings and keys to the lock for the barn door like the ones found in *THAT* Beach House in the Hamptons.

They could see Lily was nervous and frightened as she took one of the two keys and opened the door to the barn. Inside she walked to a huge chest with another lock. The second key opened it. Inside were dozens of gold bars stamped with an old railroad mark.

Dick and Jake were stunned.

"Let's get these out of here. Now. I have a real bad feeling about all this."

As they were moving the gold bars from the barn into the trunk of the car, Lily told them, "Something isn't right."

For the past hour they had moved most of the gold bars into the trunk of their rental car along with items in the canvas bag. There was also a fairly new computer behind the bag in the pantry space they also took with them.

The animals were suddenly making all sorts of noises. She could hear the small ones skittering around and the birds were flying frantically above them. Then the smell hit them.

Lily yelled, "Get out of here now. Hurry up, the barn's on fire." Dick and Jake stared at her as she shouted. "Trust me. The barn will be in flames in no time."

There was more at stake inside the barn than collecting the remaining few stolen gold bars. Their lives.

Once outside Lily called 911 from her cell phone. Still, it took at least a half hour for the fire truck and police to show up. Was it on purpose? Or was it simply small town service?

Meantime, Jake looked angrily at Lily. "Who burned down the barn and tried to kill us? What kind of crazy people do you know? First the Hamptons and now here?"

"I have no idea who's doing all this. Let's get out of here."

The police will send us a report and the real estate people will handle the sale of the farm. They're also going to find out where my aunt and uncle's dogs are and be sure they get a new home."

Dick called Dora to tell her they were driving to the Hamptons. "We'll let you know what we found when we get back. First we have a stop to make."

Dora understood, she knew her husband was being very cautious and for good reason.

Jake, Lily and Dick had spent less than five hours at the Iowa farmhouse and what they discovered were pieces of a lifetime.

A criminal lifetime.

Jake and Dick wanted Lily to give them some answers.

Chapter Fifteen
Lily's Secrets

Grabbing Lily by the arm, not exactly lovingly by any stretch of the imagination, Jake was furious. "What's going on here? We were almost killed. You have my parents and the rest of us mixed up in murders and who knows what else?"

Lily pulled away and almost in a whisper, told him and Dick, "I was sworn to secrecy when I was a teenager and shown what was in the barn. Only once. I was told there was also a canvas bag with money and official papers locked in a cabinet in the basement. Apparently, they moved it all."

"This is a mess, Lily. You must know more than you're telling us," Jake shouted.

"I've been scared half to death since my aunt and uncle were murdered. I wasn't at all sure what we would find here. It's been over ten years since I visited them and we never discussed anything about it at that time. There was a lot of silence and secrets in our family."

"Do you know where the gold and money came from?" Dick asked softly.

He was trying to ease information from Lily by being much calmer than Jake. He and Dora in their senior sleuthing career had faced even worse dangers than this. Of course, he figured it was best not to let Jake know about such things.

"Only that it was all left by my great, great uncle, James Sinclair and someday it would all be mine. I told them I didn't want any of it."

Lily was sitting on the ground under one of the large trees near the burned barn. Jake, having calmed down, sat next to her while Dick continued to ask about the money and gold they had found.

"What did they say when you told them you didn't want any of it?"

"Oh, they smiled at me, and my aunt almost sweetly said, 'Of course, dear, we understand how you feel. We felt that way too at one time. Let's not talk about it anymore.'"

"They never mentioned it to you again?" Jake was at this point mostly curious about the whole situation.

"Never. My aunt had a way of acting as if she was so sweet but over time I realized she was far more clever than my uncle and she knew how to get what she wanted. Sometimes when she was doing that he would raise his eyebrows and smile at me."

Jake pulled her closer. Lily was shivering and had tears on her cheeks. He was like his dad in that way. He had a good heart and soul. He also realized how much he loved Lily Sinclair. And he was more than a little surprised at these feelings.

Dick was standing near them, watching the police and firemen looking through the barn, now burned to the ground.

"One more thing Lily," Dick wanted to know, "how did they sound when they called you about meeting them in the Hamptons?"

"I thought they seemed rather anxious. They said it was just old age. But to tell you the truth, I didn't believe them."

***

The owners of the small Ames, Iowa real estate firm were contacted five years earlier by the Sunset Development Group. An arrangement had been made to push the Sinclairs to sell their farm and to let them know when they were going anywhere for more than a day.

That's how they knew Lily's aunt and uncle would be in the Hamptons.

***

The ride from Ames to the Hamptons included a stop in Manhattan to meet with Dick's friend, New York City Police Detective Shawn Donnelly, and have the gold bars locked safely away until they could be returned to the rightful owners. Whoever they might be.

Dick made one other arrangement.

"Frankie, I need you to meet us at MacArthur Airport. We'll return the rental car and have you drive us back to the Hamptons."

No further explanation was necessary. Everyone realized it was a smart precaution.

The canvas bag with the money and valuable papers would be transferred to the trunk of Frankie's car. He knew he had been followed.

Frankie's friends were in a black van following both cars.

Just in case!

Chapter Sixteen
The Sunset Development Group

Two men hired by the Sunset Development Group were following Frankie Socks; another had planted a bug in Dick and Dora's suite at the Beach Inn.

They were arrogant enough to think they could get away with murder and stupid enough to underestimate the people who came with Lily Sinclair to find out who murdered her aunt and uncle.

The Ames real estate office contact bragged to them, "The barn was set on fire and burned. Quite a sight. Oh yeah, we saw them loading the trunk of their car with gold bars stored inside. Who knew? That couple acted so *uppity* and religious."

"Good. Now search the house." The man on the other end was impatient with this jerk.

"We already did legally since we're the real estate company of record to sell the property."

In the small, tight-knit community of Ames, Iowa, Bradford Fulton, was known as 'Bradfullofhimself.'

"Nah. There's nothing inside of value. I found a whole lot of expired canned goods tossed about. I also expect you to let me know what happens on your end." Sounding smug, "I'll be there in a few days. After all, I need to be sure you keep your end of our bargain."

***

Bradfullofhimself didn't have a clue how dangerous the people he was involved with were. He was soon to found out.

Chapter Seventeen
Gold Deposit

"We have a trunk filled with gold bars." Dick smiled at Detective Shawn Donnelly.

"What?"

Donnelly and Dick Zimmerman had been good friends for many years and enjoyed a regular poker game together along with Zero, a newspaper reporter and owner of a nearby bar and restaurant when the Zimms were home in Manhattan. They had solved a few crimes together, well mostly murder, thanks to Dick and Dora's sleuthing.

Even when they should not have been.

Standing by the car, Dick gave him an abbreviated version of recent events, and waited for Donnelly to lead him to a place where the gold could be safely transferred and a receipt signed.

Donnelly shook his head in awe, at the sight of all the gold bars.

"I'll start checking out where they might be stolen from. I also think it would be a good idea for me to meet with Chief Saunders, he's a good man. We've met a few times. He needs to know about what you discovered in Iowa."

"Check with me in a couple of days. Sounds like a good idea."

"Stolen gold bars, hundreds of dollars of cash from who knows where, a burned barn, phones bugged, break-ins and several murders…so far. What could possibly go wrong next?"

Dick now in the back seat, Jake driving out to Long Island, laughed. "Dad, you better read up on your *Thin Man* books you like so much. You might need to do some good ole fashioned sleuthing like they did."

***

"Dora, dear, tell Frankie we should be at MacArthur Airport to turn in this car in about two hours."

"Dick, both charming and evasive, what are you up to, my dear?" Dora knew his "my dear" often meant trouble.

"Just waiting for you, darling."

Meantime, the two people hired by the Sunset Development Group to watch the beach house reported, "Two women and a man were searching the house and left with a bunch of books."

***

Dora and Cloud were talking about the books they had taken from the house.

Zero was more interested in the car following him. "Hold on, darlings, we are about to take some people on a joy ride."

The women burst out laughing as Zero put on his Indian Headdress. It had been on the floor near him. Then he began driving to the end of beach road, waving his arms in the air and blasting his horn. At the end of the road he turned around so quickly those following him almost ran into him. Zero waved and drove off before they realized what was happening.

Back at the hotel Zero suggested, "Let's get some lunch sent to the suite and you can tell me why you took those books."

The ocean spread out to their left had begun churning up, the way it always did before a big storm.

Cloud reached over to give him a kiss whispering, "Oleander."

"What the devil is oleander?" Zero quickly glanced at her shrugging his shoulders.

"Keep your eye on the road, Kemosabe," Cloud laughed.

Dora leaned over between them. She was sitting in the backseat, wondering about what it had been used for.

"Zero, love, it's a deadly poison."

Chapter Eighteen
Book Marks

Most of the books Dora took from the beach house were about murder. A few more of the books were about witches and witchcraft. A couple others were about poisons.

"Oleander?" Zero asked again, after ordering in a seafood lunch and drinks enough for a party. He figured the trio who had been in Iowa and Frankie would be arriving soon enough.

"It's a poisonous flower. A mark of death on those books." Cloud had researched the meaning of the flower and where it could be found to grow as soon as they got back to the suite.

"I've seen poisonous ones similar in the desert near the pueblo where I grew up. Just touching some of them can be deadly."

"Ever see this one?" Dora was setting the books on a table, the spines of the book with the oleander flower facing outward. Each of the books was marked by an oleander flower painted on the spine of the book.

"No. But it says it grows in many places including Iowa…and the Hamptons."

"Interesting and strange." The flower on the murder books is painted red and on the ones about witches and witchcraft it's painted white. Dora was fascinated and determined to get to the bottom of this puzzle.

"I think whoever did this was very clever. It's as if they wanted to frighten anyone who saw them. They look very threatening."

"Yeah well, whoever did it was probably a nutcase." Zero was feeling pretty darn good after his joy ride and the promise of delicious seafood.

"You're probably right. Still I think it was a nutcase with a purpose of committing murder."

Forty minutes later, two young waiters came into their suite with trays of food, drink, and serving dishes. They set up carts with everything including plates and silverware, glasses and a vase filled with flowers.

Before they left, Dora asked, "Would you please remove the flowers?"

Cloud suppressed a laugh.

***

The ocean waves began crashing loudly against the sand beyond the Inn as the three from Iowa and Frankie arrived. They were delighted to find plenty of food and drink and just as curious about the books.

Everyone had a story to tell. There was:

The gold bars in the barn.

The canvas bag filled with cash behind the expired cans in the farmhouse pantry.

The books marked with the poisonous oleander flower.

The Sunset DevelopmentGroup.

***

Dick stood up stretched and announced he was going to bed.

"It's been a long few days." Everyone else followed, stress and exhaustion had set in. Except for Frankie.

His friends left him a message. *Crisis looming. Be here tomorrow 9 am.*

Dora and Cloud agreed they would go to the local library in the morning.

"We want to do some research on the books we found at the beach house. Books eerily marked with the oleander flower on the spine." Dora told her soon to be asleep husband.

Zero and Cloud walked back to their suite. He was holding her close. Jake and Lily left right after they did, hugging his parents good night.

Reaching over to her husband of forty years, Dora sighed loudly to get his attention. "Darling, before you're completely asleep, do you think we should be concerned there could be more murders?"

"Most likely."

"Hmm, me too."

Chapter Nineteen
Definitely

Their house was several blocks from the one Lily Sinclair was set to inherit.

"We want their property. It's on almost an acre of land, we can sell it as two separate prime lots. Get rid of them. I want it done immediately so we can distract police from the beach house deaths."

This order was given by one of the people from the Sunset Development Group who ended the call with, "I want those old bastards out of there. Take care of them, then the nuisance from Iowa."

Such nice people!

He did what he was ordered to do. He always did. They paid him well. Very well in fact he once told his on and off again girlfriend. She was on again and living with him. For now.

"It's an elderly couple. The house is on Dune Road and facing the bay." Deputy Taylor had responded to a call from neighbors, concerned they hadn't seen the couple for several days.

"They walk together every morning and late afternoon. The house has been dark. I'm afraid something has happened to them. Some real estate people have been pushing them to sell."

"Where would we go if we sell? This has been our home for over fifty years." The man was nearly ninety, his wife two years

59

younger. "We bought this cottage and land before this was such an *in place to* live."

They had told their friends and their neighbors. They had no living relatives.

"They're trying to scare us, but we're not selling."

***

"Chief, I found two bodies in the small blue and white cottage on Dune Road going east. We need the coroner and forensics. They'll see the police car in the driveway."

"Taylor, check with the neighbors, find out if anyone saw anything. Don't let anyone contaminate the crime scene. I'm on my way."

"We heard a car pull away, but it was gone by the time we looked. They've been scared lately," said the neighbor in tears.

"Threats from who?" Taylor was making notes when Saunders pulled up, the coroner and forensics right behind him.

"They were threatened a lot lately."

Saunders heard her, told Taylor to tighten up the crime scene to protect it from people already driving by and staring.

"Do you know who threatened them?" Partly watching Taylor and the coroner, he was also listening to the neighbor lady.

"The real estate people lied and told the couple they owed the IRS a lot of money in taxes. They claimed they were about to lose their home so why not sell it and make some money. Oh yeah, they also promised them they wouldn't have to worry about the IRS the real estate firm would take care of it all with the sale of the property. Their card is probably inside the house. I told them it was not true."

Saunders was furious. This wasn't the first time he had heard this type of scare tactic being used on older residents. He promised himself he was going to do what he could to stop it, at least where he had some influence.

He told Taylor and one of the other officers, "Stay at the house until everyone has left, lock it up and be sure to put crime scene tape around the front and back doors. I don't want anyone in or out of here."

But in the silence of the middle of the night the tape was pulled off, the house ransacked and set on fire. It was spring and dark rain clouds hovered over the sand dunes and homes. The rain wouldn't come soon enough to help put out the fire, leaving the house burned to the ground.

When Dick heard about it on the local news, he called the police chief and then Detective Donnelly.

"The house set on fire owned by the elderly couple sounds a lot like the barn being set on fire when we were in Ames, Iowa."

Dick was a big fan of *not* believing in coincidences.

So were Saunders and Donnelly.

Calvin Osborn had his next story about elder abuse.

Chapter Twenty
Death Threats

Dick listened to the message, then played it for the others in the room.

"Bring the canvas bag you found in Iowa to *THAT* Beach House and put it in the living room. Then leave the Hamptons or one or more of you will be killed."

The muffled voice ended the call by banging down the phone. It was a little after ten in the morning.

Dick forwarded the phone message to Chief Sanders and Detective Donnelly, marked it confidential then he called and played it for Frankie Socks.

"Got it. I'm at the diner. Come here as soon as you can."

"Give us a couple hours. First Zero and I are going to visit the offices of the Sunset Development Group. They have office in town."

"Dad, what can Lily and I do?"

"Go to the attorney who notified your aunt and uncle. Find out if they've given you everything about the trust and ask if there is anything else they might have from your great, great uncle who started this mess. Lily be sure to take the copy of the will making you their one and only heir. Do not leave the original with them." Dick was clearly suspicious of them.

Lily, who had been quiet much of the time, suddenly concerned asked, "Where are Dora and Cloud?"

"Damn. They went to the library, I dropped them off there a couple hours ago," Jake answered.

If Zero the bookie would have bet they were in trouble he would be right.

***

"The research section is upstairs." An elderly man sitting at the information desk pointed to an elevator. "You young ladies need some help, let me know."

"Was he actually flirting with us?" Cloud grabbed Dora's arm leading them toward the elevator.

Dora burst out laughing. "Sure was. This is the Hamptons, seems to be in their nature."

"What?"

"Old men with younger women."

"Dora, he's old enough to be *you*r father."

"Wait, you'll see, he'll probably come up here to ask if we need anything."

Once upstairs a sign with a red arrow directed them left to a smaller room filled with research books and two computers on a long conference table.

After less than an hour, they heard footsteps heading towards them.

Dora looked over at Cloud, grinning. "Told you, he wants to help us."

This was no old man.

This was a much younger man and he had a gun pointed at them.

Chapter Twenty-One
Warned

While all this was happening the two troublesome boys who had broken into *THAT* Beach House decided to go back to rob it. Even though they had been brought back to the police station and warned they would be put in jail if they didn't stop bragging about their break in. No one ever said they were rocket scientists!

"Come on, there's a lot of good stuff we saw in there."

Parking several blocks away and each carrying a large garbage bag they walked behind the lifeless-closed houses facing the ocean.

Nearing the house, the older boy began walking faster. "Come on, let's check the basement window."

They stood staring at it, now boarded up. This time it was the younger, "genius" who grabbed his friend's arm and in hushed tones begged him, "Let's go, there's people in there."

Someone else had the same idea about looting the house.

The boys watched for over a half hour as the people inside went from room to room, carefully shining small flashlights as they quietly and efficiently took valuables.

Hearing a car start the older boy walked toward the back door of the house. "Let's see who's in there. I can take photos of them with my cell phone."

"Are you crazy? If they don't kill us, the police will. And, if they don't my folks definitely will." The younger boy was terrified. Not that it deterred his buddy already opening the unlocked door.

He should have listened to his friend.

Suddenly one man grabbed the older boy, another ran out and got the younger one. Both were beaten and warned, "Stay away and keep your mouths shut."

Almost crawling back to their car, lightning and thunder filled the sky as the two boys drove east.

"We tell our parents we were in a fight with a couple other kids. If they ask why say over a girl." The older boy's lip was bleeding and a huge lump growing on his forehead as he told this to his friend.

"Sure, but first take me to the hospital. I think I have a broken nose." Then he passed out.

***

Their parents and the police came to the hospital, the boys kept to their story. For the time being mostly because they were scared to death of what they'd witnessed. They had recognized one of the people robbing the beach house.

Meantime doing his regular check on the house, Deputy Taylor called in to Chief Saunders. "Chief, *THAT* Beach House has been robbed."

"Stay there. I'm on my way."

"Sir, it's really weird," Taylor sounded scared.

"Well leave everything alone until I get there."

Chapter Twenty-Two
Mysterious Ritual

A circle had been drawn in chalk on the living room floor of the beach house. Inside of it were a dozen different size black candles and several crosses.

"Take some photos, we sure as hell better find out who got in here and did this."

Saunders shouting orders was followed into the house by one of his other deputies. "I want you to take photos of each room, we can compare them with ones we originally took. Call forensics we need to check for fingerprints. Also, see if there's any footprints in the sand near the back door. And hurry, before it rains anymore."

"Chief, these things are used by witches. I saw a movie that had all this stuff for witchcraft rituals." Deputy Taylor seemed practically unhinged.

"What's wrong with you? You're acting crazy. Someone is just trying to scare everyone from the house."

"Well as far as I'm concerned, they're doing a damn good job of it."

"Go check the other rooms if you're not too scared." Saunders was definitely being sarcastic.

Within minutes Taylor shouted, "Chief, something is strange

in the library."

"Now what?"

"Books are missing from two of the shelves. One shelf had books about witches. I remember because they had strange markings on them and I thought how odd they looked."

"You really are an idiot. I gave Dora Zimmerman permission to come back to the house to take any books she wanted from its library. We have a list of which ones she has."

"Well, seems like someone wants us to believe there's been a mysterious ritual held in this house. We didn't see that stuff when we were here before."

Saunders shook his head, turned and walked back to the living room, when the wind suddenly blew open the front door. "Hey, Taylor, looks like there might be ghosts living here too."

Almost two hours later forensics was finished, the items in the circle bagged for evidence and the house locked with crime scene tape once again across the front and back doors.

As Chief Saunders walked toward his police vehicle, Deputy Taylor seemed convinced. "Sure looks like there was a mysterious ritual happening here."

Saunders didn't bother to reply.

***

There had, in fact, been a mysterious ritual in *THAT* Beach House, over a hundred years ago. And again, that night, apparently after the thieves left and long after the boys had been there.

Chapter Twenty-Three
Good Friends. Dangerous Enemies

"There's a hit ordered on everyone with Lily Sinclair," Frankie's friends told him.

"The Sunset Development Group are willing to do pretty much anything to get THAT beach house."

"You have people watching them?"

"Sure. But they have hired some outside help, so everyone needs to be careful and most definitely not go anywhere alone. Also, somehow, they know you have a lot of cash and information in a canvas bag you brought back from Iowa. Pretty sure there's a bug on your phone, maybe under a lamp or plant."

"Where the hell is Iowa anyhow?" asked the oldest man in the group who grew up in Brooklyn. He lived most of his life there until being sent to prison. He eventually came to eastern Long Island to live near his daughter and discovered a few of his buddies from the old days were living there too.

They began to meet once a week and stayed in touch with each other. "For old time's sake," one of them commented.

They missed the old times, but truth was, they were not old themselves.

"Listen Frankie, they're very dangerous enemies. Then again, we can be very dangerous too."

The youngest man in the group, almost 65, showed the most sinister grin.

These were men of action.

"Before you got here, we figured the following." Again it was the older of the men talking. Respect still counted for a lot with these men. They believed he deserved the respect given to him.

"Frankie, all six of your people staying at the Beach Inn will be watched at all times. We've already put some of it in place. Two people are watching the Inn where they're staying. Two of the women left before they got there. Once they show up, we'll watch after them too."

Frankie Socks nodded. They knew how grateful he was. "By the way, Iowa is where the cornfield was turned into a baseball field for old timers." He was smiling as he told them, he knew they all loved baseball. At least betting on the games at one time.

***

Dick listened to the muffled voice who demanded the bag of money found in Iowa. "We have Jake and Lily. You have two hours to get the bag of money to the beach house and leave it in the living room like I told you. Or else."

"Zero, call Saunders to come over here right away. No one else. I'll call Donnelly."

"They get hurt, I'll kill whoever harms them." Dick was in no mood to be cautious.

69

Chapter Twenty-Four
The Man From Iowa

Bradford Fulton, the real estate owner, sixty, short and with what little hair he had was in one of those ridiculous comb-over styles. Behind his back he was known as 'Bradfullofhimself.'

"Nah. There's nothing inside of value. As I told you I found a whole lot of expired canned goods tossed all over the place. We also took care of their watchdogs. Expect you to let us know what happens on your end." Sounding all braggartly and smug. "I'll be there tomorrow. I have a couple things I want to take care of here."

"Nothing to worry about." The man on the other end of the call was holding his temper. He wanted to keep Fulton calm. For now.

Being in real estate in Ames, Iowa for nearly 30 years Bradford Fulton had the opportunity to get inside many of the homes in town and farms nearby. Over the years there had been gossip about Lily's aunt and uncle having a lot of money hidden.

Fulton managed to *visit* the Sinclair farm at least a couple times a year on the pretense of someone wanting to buy a farm or some land and would they consider selling. The last time he did that a little over a year ago, he brought someone with him to take photos of the farmhouse and barn.

"Get out of here, get off our land. Don't you dare show up here again with your fake offers." Willie Sinclair was furious.

"We've put up with your nonsense for years so we could be good neighbors but coming here this time to take photos and invade our privacy is too much. If I ever see you on our property again, I'll shoot you for trespassing, that is after I have the dogs get a taste of you."

"You'll regret this, old man," Bradfullofhimself shouted as he drove away.

He had been involved with the crooked real estate people in the Hamptons hoping to get some of the money from the sale of *THAT* Beach House.

Before leaving for the Hamptons, he got into the Sinclair house one more time, found nothing in his search and of course nothing was left of the burned barn.

He reported his lack of findings then talking to himself, said, "Hell with those people in the Hamptons, I'm ready to have a *plan* of my own to get what I want. I saw them put gold bars in their car."

Chapter Twenty-Five
Jake and Lily Disappear

Bradford Fulton came to the Hamptons thinking he was going to leave a wealthy man. He was holding Jake and Lily hostage in the beach house. Thanks to his contact at the Sunset Development Group who somehow had a key and gave it to him.

They had no idea what he had planned. However, the Group knew what they had planned for him.

"Get rid of him," their enforcer was told. "Do it, sometime today. We gave him a key to the beach house. Do it there. Maybe it will scare the owner enough to sell right away." Several of them were at this meeting with him.

He knew all of them. He knew they were dangerous.

They had been paying him and his girlfriend a whole lot of money to do their dirty work. They also knew they had enough on him to own him and his silence.

***

"I know you. What do you want?" Lily shouted at Fulton who was holding a gun on them. He shoved them into the house and tied each of them to one of the dusty, moldy blue velvet dining room chairs.

Waiting for them to leave the attorney's office, he stuck a gun in Lily's back and told Jake to drive to the beach house.

"You came to my aunt and uncle's farmhouse."

"Yeah, I wanted to buy that piece of junk. I knew they had money hidden somewhere there. Now you have it, I know you do so don't lie to me." Fulton was becoming more and more irrational.

"She doesn't have any money and her aunt and uncle are dead." Jake was furious and tried to kick him.

Fulton smacked him hard across the face, cutting him with his fake diamond ring.

Lily screamed, "There's no money here. The police took it all."

"You're lying. Someone saw your family bring in a canvas bag and supposedly it has a lot of money in it. I want it."

"Please, believe me, the police took it. Said it's evidence for something. We don't know anything more about it."

"You call and get that money or your boyfriend here is dead."

Lily was stalling in hopes someone would find them. Earlier they were warned by Dick.

Dick had made them promise. "You have to stay in touch with us and call as soon as you leave the meeting." They had been warned to be very careful.

That had been over two hours ago. Jake knew his father and mother would be frantic. Dick and Dora could be tough in many ways but when it came to their boys, well, no telling what they would do to protect them. They had their own rules when it came to their children and loved ones.

Jake had once told Lily about his parents. "I think it has a lot to do with the criminals and crimes they've spent their lives fighting and knowing there's many crazy people in the world."

Jake and Lily were being confronted and threatened by one such lunatic.

"Who killed my aunt and uncle?" Lily asked, trying to keep him talking.

"Damned if I know. But I did burn down the barn in Ames. Shot their dogs too." Fulton was grinning and acting more erratic by the minute.

They heard the back door open and Fulton told them to shut up. Jake looked at Lily and went "shh." Sounding like his mother.

Fulton rushed to the back, gun in hand and started shouting, "Don't tell me I shouldn't be here. I have a key to the house."

Lily and Jake heard another voice, unsure what was being said, and then a gun shot. After that, silence.

Deputy Taylor rushed into the dining room, untied Lily and Jake and called Chief Saunders.

"Chief, I saw a car parked at the beach house. When I came in some guy tried to shoot me. He had a couple tied to chairs. One of them needs a doctor, he has blood all over his face."

Jake was also on the phone. "Dad, Lily and I are okay but—"

"What do you mean okay? Where are you and what's happened?"

Within fifteen minutes, the police chief and coroner were at the house to collect Bradfullofhimelf who was dead.

"He came at me with his gun. I had to shoot him." Taylor explained to his boss.

Minutes later Dick and Zero arrived. Jake having given his father the briefest of information on what happened.

"We were taken at gunpoint to the beach house by this crazy man from Iowa. Lily said she had seen him a few times when she visited there."

It was becoming obvious more than one someone was attempting to cause serious harm to everyone involved with the heir to *THAT* Beach House.

Lily Sinclair!

Chapter Twenty-Six
Back At The Library

The threat had been serious and sincere. Death threats tend to be that way and THAT B each House seemed to be the cause of more people ending up dead. The count of bodies was adding up.

"Go down the back stairs and keep quiet."

Picking up her purse, putting it over her shoulder, Dora didn't flinch. She knew Cloud always had a gun with her. Same as when they were kidnapped in Las Vegas and taken to The Mob Museum.

"You want our money? Here." Dora started to hand him her tote bag. She intended to use it for books and papers she would get at the library.

"Shut up, be quiet." The man pushed the gun into Dora. He was probably in his early thirties, fairly nice looking with sandy blond hair, green eyes, about Dora's height and painfully thin. Most likely from drugs or alcohol she rightfully assumed.

Cloud whispered, "Don't be ridiculous, this is a library, everyone is supposed to talk softly."

As they reached the back stairway, the old man who had flirted with them came up behind the young man.

"This youngster bothering you ladies?'

That was all it took. Cloud pulled out her gun as Dora tripped the 'youngster,' and told the old flirt, "Call the police, he tried to take us out of here at gunpoint."

Cloud burst out laughing. "You mean someone was trying to kidnap us? Again?"

It was quite a scene.

The elderly gentleman called the police, as other library staff came running upstairs to find out what was happening.

The young gunman was screaming. "They'll get you even if I didn't." Later they would be shocked to find out who had hired him.

**

Chief Saunders had them all sitting around a long rectangular table in the police station conference room. There was a large round clock on the wall ticking away the minutes while they waited.

They all started talking shouting, asking questions and demanding answers when both he and Deputy Taylor came into the room.

"Be quiet, all of you," shouted Saunders.

Dick stood up. "I'm damn angry. I don't want to be quiet. Dora and Cloud were almost kidnapped at gunpoint. Jake and Lily were taken hostage. I might add, also at gunpoint. Jake had to be treated at the hospital. It's like the Wild West here."

"You're right to be upset and alarmed. I am too. I'm adding several men to watch where you're staying. Taylor, you're to go out to the beach house now, take one of the officers with you. Be sure it's locked up front and back and put the crime scene tape across all the doors. I want one of the officers to drive by the house every hour to be sure it hasn't been removed."

Once Taylor left, Saunders leaned over the table, anger and exhaustion in his eyes. "Now, confidentially, and I do mean only us in the room are to know this, I have put other security in place with some help from your friend Frankie. We'll talk more about this soon."

Dick nodded. He understood. Then looked at the others. "Let's go."

Everyone got up to leave. They realized Dick was up to something.

Dick called Frankie Socks as soon as he was outside. "We need to meet."

To everyone else: "Stay at the Inn until I get back."

Like Dora was really going to listen to him.

Chapter Twenty-Seven
Dora

Dora had a way about her.

Intelligent and street smart, she was also stubborn and determined when she made up her mind to do something.

"I found a store about twenty miles from here that sells items for occult practices. I want to go there and find out if anyone from around here has been a recent customer."

"Mom, it's a bad idea. Dad will have a fit if you go alone."

"Oh dear, I'm not going alone. I want Lily to go with me, so I can learn more about her fun family."

"That's not funny." Jake, a large black-and-blue bruise on his face, put his arm around Lily, who gently pushed it away.

"It's a great idea. Maybe it will help us figure out what's going on."

"What's going on is people want to harm all of us. Dora, your idea is crazy." Zero was almost frantic, mostly because he knew he wouldn't be able to change her mind.

"Jake, dear, please give Lily the keys to the car and we'll be back in a few hours. You can call every hour to check on us."

***

The store was located at the far end of a small shopping center with black drapes covering the windows.

Lily asked, "Are you sure you want to go in there? Who knows what's behind those curtains."

"Well, let's find out. The worst thing that could happen is we'll be turned into frogs." Dora, smiling, was not to be deterred. Lily followed, keenly aware of Jake telling her about his mother and her affinity for getting involved in murder investigations.

"Look around. Let me know if you see something you would like to hold and see how it feels to you." A woman maybe in her early thirties invited them to explore her shop.

She was dressed in a flowing white outfit with very long, black hair, fingernails painted black and a variety of body piercings. Her face seemed kind to Dora. Her years as a judge proved her instincts were usually correct.

There were several glass cases filled with jewelry, scarves, notebooks, and more featuring occult symbols. Symbols which all held meaning to the occult practice such as the cross, the pointed star of the pentagram, the spiral representing the forever journey of life and various size black candles. Numerous versions of them also hung on the walls of the little shop.

Dora asked questions about many of the items, expressing interest, then bought a purple scarf. She hugged Lily and handed it to her. "For you, my dear."

But Lily was standing staring at a basket on the floor near the back of the store.

Paying the lady, Dora reached across the glass counter, gently taking the owner's hand. It was an interrogation technique she had learned from Dick years ago. As a criminal defense attorney, he had many such strategies he employed to seek out truth and justice.

"We're looking for someone who may have bought a lot of black candles and several crosses recently. He or she probably lives out east."

"Of course, a nice couple came by. They had never been here before."

"Do you have their names? We would like to surprise them with some similar gifts."

Who they were was the real surprise.

"Lily, we need to come another time. We promised my dear husband we wouldn't be too long." Dora wanted to get back as soon as possible with the information she just discovered.

But it was the symbol of horns on a huge basket, painted black, sitting on the counter which caused Lily to react, almost frightened. "Dora, I've seen horns like these before painted on a large crate in my uncle's barn."

"Is it okay with you if I take a few photos?"

As they were leaving the Occult shop, the lady in white held the door open for them and ever so softly, as if afraid of being heard explained, "In witchcraft, the horns are a symbol of Satan and evil."

Chapter Twenty-Eight
The Barn

"Dora, I once pried open the crate with the horns on it and inside were the gold bars. I tried to close it when I heard my aunt calling for me and knew I better get out of there."

"Was she very upset with you?" Dora hoping to learn more about Lily's family and the money, the gold and all else hidden in the barn, in Ames, Iowa.

"Both she and my uncle were very upset. Said they had told me each time I visited I was never to go in there. I lied and told them I thought I heard a cat crying and wanted to rescue it."

"Did they believe you?"

"I doubt it. There was no cat anywhere and they saw the crate with gold bars had been open."

"What did they say or do?"

"Dora, I thought it was all very strange. My aunt closed the crate, walked out of the barn with me, put the lock back on and told me to forget what happened and what I saw."

"Did you ever discuss what you saw?"

"Never. I wanted to ask her what the horns on the crate meant, but I didn't dare."

"Lily, by the way, how in the world did you manage to get into the barn if it was locked all the time?"

"I found the key. Well, after I searched the house for it while they were in town at the store." Lily took her eyes off the road for a brief minute to look at Dora with a most mischievous grin.

Dora laughed out loud. "Does Jake know this delightful side of you?"

"Well, some. He's a bit more serious most of the time."

"But he is a sweetheart, isn't he?" Dora looked at her with a mother's knowing grin.

"Absolutely!"

"By the way, Lily, didn't your aunt want to know how you found the key to the barn?"

"No. She put out her hand, I gave her the key and that was that until as I told you I was much older, and then they showed me what they had in the barn and in the canvas bag." Lily sighed and continued driving east.

***

If that was only true, thought Dora. She was deep in thought, knowing they were heading back to where there were unsolved murders, people attempting to harm her and her family, and the curious case of all that money and gold kept in the barn for so many years.

"We're heading back to where it's become more and more mysterious." Dora actually said it aloud.

Lily sighed and kept driving east to the Hamptons where it was supposedly a place of beauty, where artists and writers had long absorbed its landscape and translated it into art or poetry, of words that could never completely describe it.

Chapter Twenty-Nine
The Courthouse

"Lily, I want to make a stop." Dora was staring at the paper with the names of the two people they were told had visited the Occult shop and bought the items later discovered in the beach house.

"Zero won't be very happy," Lily commented, knowing they would do what Dora wanted.

Dora didn't respond she was making a call to an old friend.

"I know it's been a long time, but I need to see you right away."

Listening, Dora simply said, "Thank you."

"Where are we going now?" Lily sounded anxious and slightly annoyed.

"Follow the signs toward Riverhead."

"Dora, where are we going?"

"The courthouse. I was just told how to get there."

Lily said nothing at all.

Together they walked up the white steps into the courthouse, took an elevator to the third floor and into the chambers of Judge Paul Wilson.

"Lily, please call Jake, tell him we're fine and to let Zero know we'll be back soon."

When Lily reached Jake, he shouted, equally anxious and

annoyed. "Where are you? Zero is going crazy, my dad will be back soon and will probably want to send out the national guard for the two of you."

"Don't shout at me, it's your mother's idea. She insisted we come over to some place called Riverhead and meet with a judge she knows."

"What does she want from him?" Jake sounded even more frustrated.

"I have no idea, she just told me to drive here and she certainly didn't tell me why. I'm in the hallway calling you. She practically ordered me to drive here." Lily was almost laughing.

Zero had grabbed the phone from Jake. "What is going on with you two?"

"Ask Jake. I have to go. I think I'm being summoned by your Dora."

Now Zero was almost laughing. He knew THAT Dora all too well.

***

After hellos, so great to see you, it's been way too long, and all that, well plus a big hug, Dora introduced the judge to Lily.

Dora told him what had happened to Lily's aunt and uncle and everything else that had occurred since they'd arrived to help her.

"We have the names of a couple who very possibly are involved in trying to harm us. They also may or may not have murdered her aunt and uncle and some other elderly people on the east end. Do you know them?"

Dora knew Paul Wilson had been an advocate for the elderly

for the past forty years. She had always respected his work. She admired his opinions. Personal and legal.

Judge Wilson was nodding when she told them who they were. "They're bad people who act under the guise of saying they're trying to help the elderly."

"What do you also know about the Sunset Development Group?" Dora took her old friend's hand. "I believe there's going to be more murders and abuse of the elderly because they're pushing many of them to sell their homes cheap. All the properties out east are becoming worth a small fortune."

Judge Wilson sat back. He was in his robes ready for court. "Our group has been monitoring them for months. We've known they're up to no good but so far, we haven't been able to catch them doing anything illegal. They're very clever and just as careful hiding behind layers of excuses and denials."

"Have you spoken with the police?" Dora was hoping for answers even though she knew he probably didn't have all of them either

"Yes, Dora my dear, the chief of police, Saunders is a good man. He and I have spoken about this. He knows about my years of work on behalf of the elderly." Judge Wilson sighed, looking at Dora.

"Let me talk to a couple people I know who have been in discussion with me on this problem."

Judge Wilson stood up, said goodbye to Lily, gave another hug to Dora and promised, "I'll get back to you soon." She looked at his huge desk, filled with court cases, a moment of memory from the time she was a judge in Manhattan. Now amongst his papers was her card with her phone numbers and email information.

Dora was walking quickly toward the car, her mind racing

with ideas and concerns. She stopped and turned back to Lily. "Everyone okay at the Inn?"

"Sure. If you don't count Jake furious and Zero calling three times. Both more and more annoyed, and oh yes, Dick called and well, he is slightly furious with you."

"Oh, that's nothing new." Dora shrugged her shoulders and Lily thought it sounded like she almost giggled. She had.

Chapter Thirty
Planning a TRAP

Dick made it known to everyone he was less than thrilled when he heard about Dora and Lily venturing out on their own and to of all places an occult shop. Shouting over the phone to Zero, "What is Dora up to? You should have insisted she not go out alone."

Dick was ranting on and on when Zero reminded him, "You really think I could stop Lady D when she is intent on doing something?"

"I'll be back in a couple hours." Dick would have slammed the phone down if he could have, but well, today's cell phones are not made for such pronouncements.

Dick was meeting with Frankie Socks and friends.

"What now?" Dick was still too exasperated by Dora's action to have calmed down.

Chief Saunders who had joined them replied, "We set a trap."

"Whoever is behind the murders and the attempts to harm Dick and his family are not going to quit. They want *THAT* Beach House. It was built 100 years ago for a fraction of what it's worth today. They also want anything of value from Iowa."

"How do they know what we have?" Dick was still feeling quite surly about Dora and on top of it taking Lily with her.

"Bugs. In your rooms. On your phones. In your cars. We're

dealing with some very determined and not so nice people."

Frankie Socks, trying not to grin about Dora, turned to Dick. "Let's hear Saunders' idea and decide how we can help. No sense taking your frustrations out on him."

"You're right, of course, I'm sorry. Dora went with Lily to an occult shop and then over to Riverhead to meet with a judge she's known for many years."

"We know." Saunders smiled.

"Frankie's had one of his friends following them from the time they left the Inn."

This time it was Dick who burst out laughing.

"Yes, we've been alerted to Dora's penchant for taking risks. By the way, the judge she visited called me as soon as she left. He and I have been involved in a small task force to help the abused and elderly out here." Saunders was still smiling, leaning back in his seat ready to move on to the discussion about the *trap*.

An hour later, everyone had agreed on the plan and their role in it.

First step, Dick was to go with his son Jake to the Sunset Development office on the pretense of Lily being interested in selling the property she was now heir to.

"When you get back to where you're staying, take everyone out onto the beach away from people listening to the bugs they planted." Saunders was giving orders and still wanted them confidential. "Keep all this between us and your family. No one else, understood?"

"Of course, then what?" Dick was getting restless and anxious to get back.

"Tell them about the *trap* we have planned and what they'll each be expected to do."

Back at their hotel Dick followed Saunders' instructions. He also took Dora outside, gave her a knowing look, and told her about being followed, what he knew about the judge, the task force and how they would help.

Dora as always was simply charming, putting her arm through his and whispering, "Truth is, darling, I knew we were being followed."

It was the second time that afternoon Dick broke out laughing, then hugged the wife he adored.

***

Lily played her part perfectly for the first step, pretending to be yelling at Jake. Now back in their room, assuming the bugs were still in place she was acting upset and telling him, "I want to sell *THAT* Beach House. What am I supposed to do with it? I don't want to live here. It's old and needs a lot of work. Will you and your dad talk to the real estate people who came here and get an offer?"

She acted determined and sounded very convincing. "I'm serious. I want to get rid of it as soon as possible."

Jake grinned, hugged her and then called The Group to set up a meeting for the next morning.

Of course, they heard every word of her yelling about getting rid of the beach house.

The members of the group were gloating at their good fortune.

So was Lily.

Jake was truly being much more affectionate, you might even say loving, since they came to the Hamptons.

Chapter Thirty-One
Visit To The Sunset
Development Group

T he windows of the prime location that housed the
Sunset Development Group displayed photos of
nearly a dozen beautiful properties for sale. None for
less than a million dollars. They were being offered for sale by
the local real estate company several doors down from them. It
was a collaborative arrangement where the development group
appeared to be interested only in land development on the east
end of Long Island while sales were handled by others. It was
a way to make more money. In truth they were all the same
owners.

Their offices in the center of the main street were also near
two banks with numerous branches on Long Island and only
blocks from several churches, the synagogue, and the law
offices of Gibbons & Corbett.

The members of the group seemed bound together by
proximity and by their greed. None of them had any problem
with scare tactics and violence, as long as someone else did
their dirty work.

The nature of who they were at heart would become more
and more clear as things progressed. They had an extreme
sense of arrogance believing they were entitled to whatever

it was they wanted. It didn't matter to them how they got it, or even who they had to hurt to get it. Or, who had to be murdered.

All that mattered to such people was what they wanted.

The Sunset Development Group members were serious sociopaths, all had been acting on their own behalf with extreme arrogance and a sense of entitlement. Other people were simply not important to them except for what they could get from them.

Lily and Jake walked into this lion's den of welcoming fake smiles. It was the two men who had attempted to meet with Lily at the Inn and one woman from the group.

They had a round table set with flowers, coffee and baked goods so the office smelled sweet and inviting. A popular method of making a home for sale feel welcoming to interested buyers.

Lily went right into her *act*.

"I want no part of *THAT* Beach House. I—"

She was interrupted by the woman, Kathleen Barnes. The group's plan was to have Kathleen do most of the talking and appear to be compassionate about Lily's situation.

"We all understand, dear. All of this has to be such a shock to you." Oh, Kathleen was very good.

So was Lily. "Yes, you're right. I appreciate your kindness."

Jake took Lily's hand. "Why don't you tell us what Lily needs to do to sell the house. As we understand it according to my parents, she is not yet the formal owner."

"True. For now, we will provide you with a contract from our company agreeing to buy the house from Lily, for fair market value. She is after all the rightful heir and owner." Kathleen was great at double talk.

"Jake, what do you think, sweetheart?" If Lily sounded any more like a meek, vulnerable young women he would have burst out laughing. She most definitely was not. In all the years they had been together, he knew her to be strong and confident. It was certainly some of what he admired about her. Of course, there were other things. He was very much aware of the courage and confidence she had displayed during this crazy ordeal.

"If you're sure this is what you want to do, it sounds fine." The three people from the group were ready to pounce.

Believing they had Lily Sinclair right where they wanted her, Kathleen went into her act again. "As for price, Lily, anyone who buys it will probably want to tear it down and build a new house."

"Really? Why?" Lily sounding surprised even appearing to be dumbfounded by her suggestion.

"Well, the floorboards, roof and probably elsewhere are rotting. The police only allowed us a quick look, but chances are since there was no building code to speak of when it was built, there's probably asbestos and mold in the walls." Kathleen was on a roll.

"Oh dear, it certainly sounds bad." Lily acted shocked. Truth was at this point she wanted to just get away from these terrible people.

"How much are you offering Lily for the house?" Jake's question seemed to surprise them. They had wanted to slow walk their incredibly low offer.

Lily leaned and put her elbows on the table and folded her hands, careful not to touch anything on it.

One of the men gave her a number.

As Lily asked, "How long will it take you to get a proposal in writing for me?" Kathleen pushed a contract in front of Lily.

"We knew how anxious you sounded to sell so we prepared this in advance for you. Sign it and we'll take care of the rest." Really, how much more charming could Kathleen Barnes be?

Surprising Kathleen and the two men, Lily stood up, contract in hand and acted flustered. "I better let Jake's parents read this over."

Kathleen tried to take it back from Lily. She didn't want anyone to see the contract showing they were virtually stealing the property by offering much less than it was worth.

"Well why don't you just tell them about the offer, and we'll meet you here again tomorrow morning." Kathleen, now more than a bit frantic as she tried one more time to get the contract back.

Lily had her bag over her shoulder, Jake with his arm around her as if protecting her, told them, "We'll see you tomorrow."

What the Sunset Development Group didn't know was Lily was wearing a wire. Also, Jake carefully planted a bug under the table, given to him by Saunders, in their office, where they had made the ridiculous offer they expected Lily to accept right then and there.

***

Dick and Dora had listened to the conversation. So did the police chief and the editor of the local paper. Zero and Cloud were out wanting some alone time.

"We need to decide what we'll do when we leave here," Zero had earlier told Dick. Meantime they were there to help Lily and Jake.

Osborn had already written a frontpage story about Elder

Abuse to be published in the paper the next morning.

Over the next 24 hours the Sunset Development Group would reveal a great deal of information to those listening in...and taping it.

They would expose their real selves, their real ambitions and their real agenda. Still finding the murderers was a top priority.

Chapter Thirty-Two
Front Page

Above the fold, on the front page of the morning paper a story about elder abuse being a national disgrace, was presented in heartbreaking detail with personal stories.

They are harmed and abused financially, emotionally, physically, and even sexually, usually by caretakers, sometimes including relatives, who are responsible for their well-being. According to reports half a million seniors are abused each year. And those are only the ones reported.

Having the editor of the paper feature this story on the front page was the next step in the planned trap. The intention was to make the development group realize it was possible someone was watching and aware of what they were doing to remove the elderly from their homes through harmful tactics.

The judge agreed to call Calvin Osborn as soon as he was told about what was being planned. "I need a favor." He gave him an update on the Elder Abuse Task Force. I have several people for you to interview for another story."

Without mentioning names, Osborne printed the stories he had been told.

"My parents were threatened and bullied almost every week until they finally sold their house because they feared for their lives."

"She died in a nursing home where she was supposed to be cared for but instead, we discovered she had been sexually abused, usually, in the middle of the night, by another resident. When she told the people who worked there, they didn't believe her. There was an autopsy after she died, and it showed recent sexual activity."

"She's almost twenty-five years younger than our father. She spent a fortune on clothes and jewelry, wrote checks, signing his name and physically abused and threatened him. He was too scared and well, also embarrassed, to tell us until we found him lying in bed with bruises all over his body."

Osborne had far too many stories to choose from, it was heartbreaking to read them.

The editor requested, "Judge, can you give me a quote for the story?"

Judge Paul Wilson has told this paper anyone brought into his courtroom and found guilty of elder abuse can expect a severe sentence.

In addition, Chief of Police Art Saunders has promised The local police are following up on all reliable leads regarding the recent murders of seniors related to various scams and scare tactics. There are many stories and examples of this disgraceful behavior.

Attempts have been made to force them to sell their homes. A senior couple, here from Iowa told they were the heirs to a large beach house, were murdered in their van. Their family has plans to hire a criminal attorney to check into their deaths.

Dora was reading the article aloud. Of course, they had all read it, now they wanted to discuss what was happening next. What they really wanted was for those who were listening in on their conversations to hear their thoughts about it.

"Dick, go with me to the beach house. There's a few more books there I want to get." Dora picked up her tote bag and waited for him to reluctantly agree.

"Fine, but Saunders will have to meet us there to let us in."

They made the call to Saunders and headed to the beach house in the car. Dora explained to Dick, "I really just want to do some sleuthing, dear, and out of earshot from our nosey intruders."

"Why? What do you expect to find? A couple broomsticks?" Dick loved teasing his wife, knowing at times like this she most surely had an agenda.

"I haven't told any of you yet, but I found several lengthy letters written by Lily's great, great uncle, James Sinclair, in one of the books we got from his library." Dora pulled them out of her tote bag, smiling.

"Why not tell any of us?" Dick parked in front of the beach house.

"They're very incriminating and prove he was a murderer. I figure Lily has been dealing with enough for now." Dora handed Dick one of the letters. When Saunders arrived, she slipped it back in her bag.

Chief Saunders and Dick stood outside in the sunshine as Dora went into the dark and creepy house. The house itself seemed to have died over the years it was locked without any human life inside it.

Waiting for Dora, Saunders and Dick discussed the frontpage article.

"Why do think there's so much elder abuse? You were an attorney for many years experiencing all kinds of terrible human behavior."

"I think the paper has a good focus on it. Greed, revenge, money, did I say greed?" Dick handed it to Saunders who had of course already seen it.

What are the causes of elder abuse? Many. Caretakers get stressed out and it turns to anger. Some nasty situations relate to finances including caregivers. Stealing money, writing checks, misusing funds. There are phony investments and charities. There are also those in the medical profession who are unethical and unprofessional when it comes to their older patients.

"Well I'm impressed with the article, especially the last paragraph," Dora commented as she walked out of the beach house holding several books and a photograph of Lily's great, great uncle. There were none she could find of his wife or her sisters.

Dick and Chief Saunders agreed, the last paragraph was an important and powerful message.

Maybe we can't stop all of it everywhere. Maybe there will always be cruel people who abuse the elderly. Maybe there are some who are even your friends or neighbors, your business associates, or members of your community. I believe if we can stop some of it out here, the message will spread elsewhere. So, please take action, if you know someone, anyone who is doing harm to an elderly person or persons, please, tell the police, tell this paper and help stop it. Now!"

Step two, done.

Chapter Thirty-Three
Panic

The prominent politician involved with the Sunset Development Group demanded, "We need to meet tonight, seven p.m. at your office."

He clearly was in a state of panic after being contacted by a New York City reporter planning on doing a follow up story on elder abuse after reading the one in the Hampton paper.

Of course, that was part of the plan, part of the trap.

The other members agreed to meet.

They had a right to be concerned about what could happen to them if the ugly truth was exposed. It was easy enough to know the names of the members when the group was first formed there was a very different article in the paper about them and their 'promise' to bring good development plans to the east end. That was over five years ago and how times had changed.

"If the police or press find out we've been behind much of this we'll all go to jail," warned the politician.

"How could someone so savvy be so stupid?" Everyone thought the same thing as Dick and Dora with everyone including Saunders listened for two hours. Thanks to the bug Jake put under the table in their office.

There was no shortage of blame. The group talked about what had been done and what they should do to protect themselves. They seemed to have no problem with murder and when they talked about who committed them on their behalf, it truly shocked everyone listening to their conversation. Their brilliant plan was to put all the blame on them.

In the meantime, Dora had read the contract they offered Lily for the purchase of the house. "It's shameful."

She handed it to Dick to read. When he was finished, he tossed it on the coffee table in front of him. "Actually, I think it's illegal. Even though Lily is the rightful heir, there are some legalities required before she becomes the owner of *THAT* Beach House."

***

The next day Dick made a stop at the group's office on the pretense of asking a few questions about the sale of *THAT* Beach House. His real purpose was to remove the listening device his son Jake had placed under the table in their conference room the day before.

Dora was telling everyone else what was in the letters she found from Lily's great, great uncle Sinclair. Many were hidden in the books on murder. Several were in the books on poison. She had found many more of them hidden in the back of the picture frame with his photo.

"He had underlined sections of many of the books. He wanted us to find out what he did. He was quite proud of his plan and ability to carry it out."

Dick had discussed all this the night before with Dora, after everyone left. After everyone had listened to the group's revealing meeting.

"Lily needs to know all this, dear. It will help her understand what's happened and why. By the way how did you know those letters were behind his photo?"

"Sort of deductive reasoning. Why did he have a photo of himself setting on a table for everyone to see and none of anyone else? It was like an invitation to hear from him."

Dick hugged Dora and turned out the light, put his arms around her and asked her, "Are you tired?"

Chapter Thirty-Four
About The Letters

Found in the books marked with poisonous flowers were sections underlined providing murderous ideas of Lily's great, great uncle James Sinclair. He painted a small oleander flower on the spine of the books. Red on the murder ones and white on the other books.

He wanted people to believe his wife and her two sisters had their bodies and souls taken over by witches and they had to be destroyed. His plan was to kill them and lock them away in death the way he felt locked away in life by them.

The letters written over a period of a few months were an admission of what he had done. He bought *THAT* Beach House in the Hamptons because of it being far away from Ames, Iowa. The letters were a true confession of a man who did terrible things and an explanation of why, where he got the money, the gold and more.

I bought the land 1916. It took several years to build the beach house. I wanted it as an essential part of my plans to relieve myself of marriage and my sisters-in-law who lived with us. By the time anyone reads these letters I expect years and generations will have passed. My heirs will be told in my will what they are to receive.

Some of you will be grateful for being left with a great deal of money and valuables. Others probably somewhat disgusted. It matters not at all to me how you feel about me and what I've done. My need to escape took hold of me mentally and physically. I became a thief, a liar, a scoundrel of sorts and well yes, a murderer. Why not?

I married young since I was in desperate financial need. I hated my wife-to-be from the moment we met. She was spoiled, pretentious and demanding. Her looks did not appeal to me and we ultimately agreed to spend little time on any romantic endeavors. In and out of bed. It was not surprising we had no children.

My wife's mother and two older sisters lived with us after our marriage. My mother-in-law died unexpectedly after living with us for less than two years. No surprise there either. Not for me anyhow.

I sent her off the same as I had my own vicious mother.

It was the beginning of changing my life even though it would take some time to finish. I was normally not a patient man but my decision of what I wanted to do required careful planning and time, lots of time, almost eight years from when I eliminated my mother-in-law from living with us.

*As I said, I do mean not **living** with us!*

Chapter Thirty-Five
1916 In Ames, Iowa

A s I said, I'm normally not a patient man. But this decision for me to change my life required a great deal of patience. First, I was aware I would require a lot of money. To that end I became close friends with the head of the bank.

When I learned a large gold shipment going from the east coast to the west would spend the night in his bank, I knew I had indeed struck gold. Without giving you all the gory details, I robbed the bank. I took the gold bars and all of the money in the vault. There was close to a quarter of a million dollars. I set it up to look like the bank manager was responsible. He was later hanged.

Clever, don't you think?

Now, I had previously purchased several items in preparation for this windfall. I set upon putting a new lock on the barn door and placed two large trunks that looked like wooden crates inside the barn.

While we did live on what was considered farmland in Iowa, we were not farmers. Far from it. My wife's family would not stand for such an indignity. We entertained their friends, had dinners and cocktail parties, went to dances and other celebrations. Our home was considered a country cottage decorated with beautiful furnishings. Both the home and all in it were purchased by my in-laws. However, I demanded they be in my name if I agreed to the marriage.

There was a large barn on the farmland. I bought a lock for it which could only be opened with a special skeleton key I had made. I had another skeleton key made for the crate with the gold bars in it. I knew my wife and her sisters would never consider going into the barn and it was far enough from the house they paid it no mind.

Next, I set about purchasing land in the Hamptons and built the house one of you now owns. I am sorry for the dead bodies you've discovered. But well, life has its challenges, doesn't it?

One day, I started to pretend to cough a lot, complaining and sighing about it. I held my chest and tears ran down my cheeks. I kept at what I thought was a brilliant performance and after many months I told everyone it was advisable for me to live near an ocean where the sea air would be good for my lungs.

My ideas about a special poison flower I figured would help take care of their lungs.

And so, I built the beach house after finding a perfect piece of property facing the ocean and miles from any other homes.

My wife and her sisters were very unhappy about this decision. We finally agreed once the house was ready, we would spend half the year there and half in Iowa.

Of course, I knew I was never going to live back in Iowa again with them.

Before we left for the beach house in the Hamptons, I made sure all was secure in the barn. I planned to come back once a year to refill my own cash needs and take a gold bar or two. I figured it would be very dangerous to travel west with so much money.

Once we arrived in the Hamptons, settled in and I felt comfortable I began to add small amounts of oleander poison to the evening cocktails of my wife and her sisters.

106

The poison came from the oleander flower. I had purchased some seeds and carefully planted them behind the barn in Ames. After only weeks, they were all feeling ill, listless and crying to go back to Ames complaining they felt too sick in the beach house.

Really, it was simple. I know you must think I'm a monster. But, honestly, they felt very little when I strangled them to death thanks to the poison in their systems.

For days after all three were dead, I filled my library with books I had bought about murder and witchcraft I had hidden from them. For any of you reading my letters now will enjoy, I truly believe, searching through these books for more letters and my markings in them. I discovered horns were symbols of Satan and drew them on one of the crates in the barn. I felt like living with them was like living with Satan!

And finally, I had a second key to the barn made. I'm leaving it in my wife's personal clothing drawer. Clever, don't you think?

Do what you wish with all that's left. The house, any money or gold.

I would burn the house down, however, it seems more symbolic of how I feel, to let these three women rot in it for the next 100 years.

You may think I'm the one who should have been left to rot in it. But we know, life isn't always fair.

Chapter Thirty-Six
The Canvas Bag

T he legal and financial papers along with old newspaper clippings provided additional insights into Lily's great, great uncle, James Sinclair, and the years following his heading west for a new life. The law firm for the trust also had copies of these same papers and the will.

Family members had saved them and passed them on to each heir receiving the farmhouse, the beach house, and the money. Some used some of the money but were too scared to risk using a gold bar for any reason. They knew there would be questions they couldn't answer. Like where the gold came from. That answer was in the locked beach house.

The last of course were Alice and Willie Sinclair. The only difference being they were heirs when the 100-year trust was ready to pass along the title to the beach house.

"Now I understand how my aunt and uncle were able to be so generous to my father and me. All those expensive gifts they gave us year after year." Lily was reading a journal detailing the money they took from the canvas bag. In addition, they put $25,000 of it in a bank account for Lily as part of their will.

Dick and Dora listened as Lily and Jake discussed what to do with all of it.

"Jake, I can't and don't want to keep any of this. I'm not sure what to do with it."

"Lily, let's get through what's happening here in the Hamptons and my folks will help us figure it out. I'm sure they already have some ideas."

Dora got up and gave her son a hug. She adored him, it was so obvious. "Both of you, we do have some ideas."

Meantime, the gold bars were safe in police storage in Manhattan. Detective Donnelly would arrange for the return of the gold bars to the rightful owners. Whoever they might be.

The media went crazy over the story. After all it was filled with intrigue, mystery, murder and more than a million dollars of gold according today's market value.

As for the poisonous oleander flowers planted behind the barn in Ames, Iowa, when the barn was set on fire and burned to the ground, they went with it. Afterwards neighbors wondered for days about the strange odor.

Chapter Thirty-Seven
The Occult Shop Call

"They just left."

The shop owner promised to call Dora if the couple whose photo she showed her returned to buy more witchcraft items.

"What did they buy?" Dora began writing a list of the items.

"Isn't this a lot? Seems like they're planning a big event?"

"I thought so too, but when I said something the woman got very nasty," the shop owner told Dora, adding, "I thought this was strange. Most people buy a few items at a time if it's for a ritual."

"How did they pay, cash or charge?" Dora wanted to know.

"That was strange too. They spent at least ten minutes arguing back and forth what was the best way to pay. The man wanted to charge it, the woman said cash was best so it couldn't be traced."

"Did they say anything about what they were planning?"

"They kept whispering. To be honest, I tried not to hear but they kept getting louder and louder saying something about later at the beach house."

Dora hung up, then told everyone else what she had just heard. Shaking her head, she muttered, "Fools planning acts of desperation."

Everyone agreed, the couple was up to something incredibly stupid and foolish.

Chapter Thirty-Eight
The Judge's Opinion

"Our taskforce will see to it that anyone abusing the elderly or using any type of scare tactics on them will be punished to the full extent of the law. I know I've said this before, but I don't think I can say it enough, you bring peril to the elderly, you bring it to yourself."

Judge Paul Wilson gave the comments for a follow-up article to be on the front page of the next day's paper.

There was an outpouring of letters to the editor sent by text and email demanding those who harmed the elderly be arrested and prosecuted to the full extent of the law.

They could not deny being in the line of fire. They, being the Sunset Development Group.

In the second meeting in two days, the group decided. "We need to pull back. No more offers to buy homes until all this calms down. Call your man and tell him to step back. We don't want him making any threats or starting any more fires."

"He's not easy to handle," one of the group warned.

"Tell him it's for all our protection. Things will quiet down soon enough and then we can move forward with our plans," another commented.

Wishful and arrogant thinking was certainly part of their

stupidity.

Dick and Dora Zimmerman had spent a lifetime fighting injustices, each in their own way. Zero had been a part of their lives for most of his life. And Frankie Socks was around to protect them many a time in recent years. Like now.

Frankie Socks and his friends met with everyone helping Lily in a quiet out of the way restaurant away from listening ears to make their plans.

"I think we've anticipated as much as possible." Dora looked at him with a sly grin.

Dick looked around the table, all people he cared about. "Now, you don't think I would trust them to come without their wanting to do us harm."

Lily, alarmed, asked, "Will we be alright?"

"My parents know what they're doing. I trust they have a plan in place for protecting us." Jake clearly had great faith in his mother and father.

"Absolutely. Which is why Frankie Socks is here," Dick added. Frankie just nodded.

"I've asked him and his friends to, shall I say, be on the alert." Suddenly Cloud asked, "What does that mean?"

Zero called the waiter over for another round of drinks, then responded, "Don't ask!"

After that, no one did.

Step three was about to take place.

Chapter Thirty-Nine
Fools

Earlier in the day, Dick and Dora, our favorite senior sleuths set the third step of the plan in motion.

"I do believe it's time for a good old-fashioned reception for some of the lovely people we met out here this visit." Dick was smiling at Dora.

"Darling, I think you're quite right. The police chief said he will help with the invitations and added police presence." Dora went over and hugged her husband and best friend.

Dick continued with the playfulness which helped to ease the stress and tension of the past week and next step of the trap.

"Shall we say invitations are mandatory?"

"Absolutely, dear. We wouldn't want anyone to miss the fun."

"Okay you two, enough, what are you up to?" Zero laughing knowing it would be fascinating. They had all discussed planning a trap to catch the criminals, a few details were left to Dick and Dora until now.

"We'll need all of you to help plan a little party for tomorrow evening." Dick picked up the phone and confirmed it with Saunders, then contacted Detective Donnelly.

Dora called and invited Judge Wilson. "I don't think you'll want to miss this."

"You're right. Email me the details and I'll be there." He hung up.

Then she called Calvin Osborne and Carlton Gladstone, the NYC reporter who also had written recent stories on elder abuse. Both said they wouldn't miss it.

Neither would Frankie Socks and friends. They would be around the property being sure no funny business was going on.

It turned out to be a damned good thing.

***

While Dick and Dora made calls, Zero and Cloud, along with Jake and Lily arranged for champagne, champagne glasses, and the location. There would also need to be folding chairs and plenty of candles.

It was to be at **THAT** Beach House at six p.m.

Most accepted the invitation without a fuss. A couple made a big fuss. But really what choice did any of them have?

***

There were many quotes about fools.

The two fools who bought the witchcraft items intended to create a diversion and set their own drama in motion, thinking they were smarter than everyone else.

"We'll have to do it late, once this ridiculous so-called cocktail party is over," she told her partner.

"Agreed. We'll need to get him to help us set the fire. He did a great job burning down that old couples house."

They were soon to be the biggest fools of all.

Chapter Forty
Exposed

They were "invited" to be at *THAT* Beach House. Well, more like commanded to by Police Chief Saunders.

The event was to take place in the living room, where once again a circle had been drawn in chalk. Only this time it was done by Dick and Dora. They had Lily and Jake lighting candles throughout the room fifteen minutes before the drama was to begin.

"They're either belligerent, arrogant, or simply annoyed," Zero whispered to Cloud as the so-called guests arrived.

Zero and Cloud were responsible for welcoming the unhappy guests. Zero promised Dick he would not wear his Indian Headdress that evening. He also told Dick he owed him big and you can bet, which Zero loved to do, he would collect.

Police officers were at the front and back doors to prevent anyone from bringing in a weapon or leaving.

Candles gave light to the room since wiring in the old house did not provide modern electricity. Folding chairs were placed around the chalk circle.

"Please be seated." Dick pointed to where he wanted each person to sit and smiled so graciously it was impossible for anyone to figure out what he was up to.

Saunders raised his eyebrows and turning away from the

guests told Donnelly, "I hope he really knows what he's doing."

"He usually does." Donnelly smiled. "Wait and watch." Unlike some of the others, Donnelly had plenty of previous experience with Dick and Dora to know they were certainly no fools.

As the last person to join them was seated, the doors were locked, and Saunders told anyone complaining, "Shut up or you'll be arrested."

Seated were the members of the Sunset Development Group

The two men and woman who owned the real estate company sat next to each other. Next to the woman was Jonathan Gibbons, lawyer from the firm that created the trust. The politicians and the trustee from the synagogue sat across from them. Lily sat next to Gibbons with Jake on her other side.

Judge Wilson said he preferred to stand.

There were seats for Dick and Dora and an empty one near one of the politicians.

Unfortunately, it stayed that way.

"May I say how delighted we are you could join us." Dick was so gracious, but no one smiled, well, except for Zero. He knew what was coming.

"Five people have been murdered, a house burned to the ground, homes robbed, and other unscrupulous tactics engaged in, all meant to scare the elderly. Some were also meant to force Lily Sinclair to sell this house. Lily and my son were held hostage by a mad man a few of you did business with for a number of years. Of course, by business I mean he kept you informed about Lily's aunt and uncle and the farm they owned in Ames, Iowa. He too has now been murdered."

Dick looked around the room, watching the guests' body language and continued. "By the way, the local police in Ames have determined he set fire to their house and barn and killed their dogs. One of the people who worked for him, an old friend of Lily's confessed to everything."

"I'm leaving. I never did any of those things. I'll sue the lot of you," one of the politicians stood up and shouted, only to quickly be put back in his seat by Saunders.

"You are all involved, in one way or another, by actually committing the crime, or by providing the group with funding. We know for a fact, the Sunset Development Group wanted to buy up as much land on the east end as cheaply as possible, then sell it for a great deal more. You were willing and did whatever it took to accomplish your greedy ambitions."

Lily suddenly yelled at the group, "You're all awful, you killed my aunt and uncle."

Dora looked at Dick. "Darling, perhaps we should let them know we do have plenty of evidence of their wrong doings."

"Yes, dear, you're quite right."

The woman real estate owner cursed them and promised, "I'll sue you for all you're worth. How dare you accuse us with these lies and clearly a whole lot of nonsense."

"Kathleen Barnes thinks we're bluffing. For one thing, my dear, we know you're also an attorney with the firm Gibbons & Corbett. By the way, we have a lovely photo of you and Jonathan Gibbons taken at the occult shop purchasing witchcraft items."

"You miserable people, you'll all be sorry." Kathleen Barnes certainly was not very happy about this information.

Dora continued, "All of you wanted the beach house so badly because you know it's worth a fortune in today's real estate market. So badly in fact, you arranged for another elderly couple to be killed in an attempt to confuse us and the police—"

Dick interrupted, "A distraction you hoped would keep the police so busy, they wouldn't have the time or resources to pay attention to the other murders. But they did and we have been only too glad to assist."

Dick was no longer smiling. He was accusing the members of the Sunset Development Group of criminal acts, including murder.

Saunders suddenly called Dick over for a minute and whispered to him, then sent out two police officers with orders. "Find him and arrest him."

Dick took a moment to talk to Saunders, then went back and continued talking to the people sitting around the chalk circle. "We do have a witness. He confessed to his role in setting the fires, murdering all five people and using the scare tactics frightening so many elderly people these past few years. We have video tape of his confession explaining how he was ordered to do these things by the Sunset Development Group."

The synagogue lady said, "I know nothing of this."

The politicians pleaded complete innocence.

The others sat in silent terror aware they were in big trouble.

"Chief, would you like to comment?" Dick turned toward him with a knowing nod.

Saunders moved closer to the people sitting in the room, telling them, "Not only do we have a taped confession, but the person you hired to do these terrible criminal acts protected himself. He has kept copies of anything you emailed or texted him. Oh, and he taped all your meetings and phone calls."

Just then one of the police officers walked back in and whispered to Saunders.

"I have to go. He's on the run. Dick, my officers will take everyone from the Sunset Development Group into custody. Donnelly, I could use your help getting them to the police station."

"Consider it done. Would you prefer I go with you?" Donnelly was more than a little concerned for Saunders' safety as he was going after a murderer.

"No. I want this one myself. He's going to spend the rest of his life in jail if I have anything to do with it. Judge, I'm hoping you'll make it happen."

Wilson nodded as Saunders left. He knew who was being pursued.

A politician commented, "I've left a message for my attorney. You'll regret this."

He didn't sound very confident as another of the guests expressed her determination to leave.

"I want to know who the hell you think is the person we supposedly hired to set the fires and commit the murders." The woman from the synagogue had begun shouting. "I'm leaving, just try and stop me."

Donnelly grabbed her as she ranted and raved and tried to go out the front door.

"I believe our little get together is over, darling. Seems the guests do want to leave."

Dora grinned at what she thought of as the madding crowd and went to stand by Lily and Jake.

The next half hour was almost like a cartoon film with people being told to get moving, some cursing and fighting it, others resigned to what was happening. Judge Wilson and the two newspaper people left having said nothing. They would have plenty to say in the next day's papers including the judge who would be quoted about the expansion of the task force for the elderly.

The party planners were exhausted.

"I want a steak and a drink," demanded Zero.

"Me too, my good man. As soon as we clean up here." Dick and Zero both laughed.

Dora and Cloud began blowing out the candles and just shook their heads as Jake and Lily put the folding chairs against the wall.

But it would be a while yet.

The "hit" man, Deputy Earl G. Taylor was on the run with his girlfriend and clearly with violent intentions. He was not going to take the blame alone for the actions he had been hired to do.

Chapter Forty-One
Deputy Taylor On The Run

Deputy Taylor was on the run as the meeting at the beach house was taking place. He was the one who'd left the empty chair.

Obviously familiar with the police station after more than three years serving as a policeman, he had quickly figured what would be his best chance for escaping.

Saunders and the community would certainly not consider what he had been doing as serving anyone but himself.

Brought to the police station the morning before the meeting at the beach house Deputy Taylor knew the exact moment he would be able to shove the policeman taking him into a cell. He would rush down a narrow hall leading to a door opening to an alleyway.

Handcuffs were of no concern to him. He had a key to handcuffs and his car sewn inside the lightweight jacket he had been wearing. He once told his girlfriend "I keep a set of these in all my jackets in case they ever catch up with me." This was his big precaution in case he was arrested for murder? He was a fool. Like those who paid him to destroy **THAT** Beach House.

"Take these items and remember to leave them all around

the house when you're finished." It was the same woman who purchased all the witchcraft items. Stuffing them in the trunk of his car he told her, "I'll be at that meeting tomorrow evening with the chief. Pretend you don't know me."

So, it was understandable Taylor had been shocked when Saunders arrested him the next morning. "What is this about? I haven't done anything wrong."

"Cut the bull, Taylor. We've heard some interesting conversations lately. One of our officers installed listening devices in the offices of the Sunset Development Group and Gibbons & Corbett Law Firm. You're their go to guy for almost anything illegal they want done. Good thing they paid you a hefty fee since you're going to need a good attorney." Chief Saunders was clearly and utterly disgusted with his deputy.

Smug and leaning on his elbow on the table where he had interrogated many people Taylor laughed. "You never realized they were the ones who helped me get this dumb job so I could be out here to work for them."

Reaching over the table, pulling on Taylor's jacket, Saunders snapped at him, "You moron. You think any of it matters? Do you think they care at all about you? You're going to jail for the rest of your life with little hope for any leniency. Unless…."

The smug look still on Taylor's face, he stared at the chief of police. "Unless what?"

"You give us everything you know about the people you've been working for since you've been in the Hamptons." Saunders sat back; he was the one with the smug expression now.

Detective Donnelly knocked on the door of the interrogation room. He had arrived for the beach house party early so he could join Saunders at the station.

Donnelly and two officers sat with Saunders and listened to

Taylor tell them what he had done for his employers. He also had them get a locked box under his bed in his apartment only blocks away from the village.

"In it is all the proof you could ever want. I saved all their emails, taped all our conversations. You don't think I ever trusted those S.O.B.s do you?" Taylor was showing off, thinking how smart he was.

He was still figuring out how he could escape and handle the job they wanted him to do that evening. Not so much for money, but for revenge. He hated everyone at that moment.

***

Dick and Dora were far along with their accusations event at the beach house when Saunders was told Taylor had escaped. After telling Dick "When I catch him, I'm putting him in jail and throwing away the key. Saunders was furious. Oh, they would catch him, but first there would be even more drama before the night was over.

Chapter Forty-Two
THAT Beach House

There was a full moon although most of it was covered by dark clouds floating over it as if they had to be somewhere important. Still, there was enough to give some light on the beaches, and dunes of the Hamptons.

And, on **THAT** Beach House.

Which is where Deputy Taylor was headed. Driving on side roads leading to the house he parked in the driveway of a house not too far away. He knew it was not yet opened for spring and summer. He always knew which ones weren't opened. It meant they were prime targets for stealing things left in them year-round.

He and his girlfriend had been doing that for the past few years.

He took the bag of witchcraft items out of his trunk along with a flashlight and matches for the candles.

When she had handed him the bags, she told him, "You know what you're to do. Get it done before midnight. Everyone should be gone by then. We expect to be in the Village Bar & Grill, so we'll have an alibi and can't be blamed."

Little did she know what was in store for them that evening.

Taylor walked quickly along the beach. The ocean was

stirring up from the heavy winds and almost all the houses facing the ocean were dark and quiet. It would all change soon. Summer and the onslaught of homeowners and tourist taking over was only a couple months away.

The beach house was cleared of everything for the 'party' and the doors and windows closed and locked. Dick and Dora, friends and family had left.

"I've had enough of those people. Let's go eat and decide where we want to go from here." Dora put her arm through Dicks, leaned over and kissed him.

Within fifteen minutes they were being served drinks.

Their conversation covered the events of the evening and ideas for where everyone might go.

"Paris said Jake." Lily, surprised, hugged him.

"New Mexico, we have some unfinished business there," Cloud told everyone.

"Guess I better get my headdress ready to wear," Zero laughed.

"Yes, you better." Cloud sat there sipping her second glass of wine.

Everyone was in need of a cocktail or two at this point. Dick and Dora hadn't suggested where they might go. They felt like anything was possible. They had an apartment in Manhattan, one in Las Vegas, and the means to go anywhere they wanted.

A week later something would dictate where they would go after leaving the Hamptons.

Frankie Socks would of course go back to Manhattan. Always home to him, even when he was in the Witness Protection Program. In his heart it was home.

For now, this evening of accusations and arrests, Frankie and his friends watched all around the property until everyone

Dick cared about left THAT Beach House. He saw them get in their cars and drive away. It was time for him and his friends to go too.

They had arrived together in one of the men's van. Frankie's car left parked by the police station, figuring it would be safe there and knowing there was not much room to park by the house.

Dick told him earlier about the evening events and thanked him and his friends for their help finding information about Deputy Taylor.

An important piece of information they had brought to Saunders was the admission from the two boys who had first broken in the beach house. "Deputy Taylor beat us after we found him and his girlfriend robbing the house. Told us he would kill us if we said anything."

Later, Taylor's girlfriend was arrested for aiding and abetting him with his crimes including murder. She too would be going to prison for a long time. She too after much cursing gave up her man!

It had been quite a week for everyone.

Old buddies, Frankie and his friends sat in the van joking and reminiscing.

Suddenly he told the others in the van, "Be quiet. I think hear someone by the house."

"Maybe just the ocean churning up," one of the men suggested.

Frankie was hesitant. "Probably. But let's wait a few minutes."

Another person was now opening his door. "Let's go check, I hear something too."

It was then the sky glowed yellow and red with black smoke from the rear of the house. Flames started shooting upwards and it seemed as if the old house was going to explode.

Frankie shouted to the driver of the van, "Call 911! We'll need fire and police here."

Everyone else in the van got out and ran to the back of the house with him. Tossing the witchcraft items the couple had given him around the back of the house stood Deputy Taylor.

"See, witches stared the fire. See, see, see." Taylor was screaming and laughing hysterically like a crazy person. He had set the house on fire. He knew what he was doing. It wasn't the first fire he had set in the Hamptons.

He fought off two of Frankie's friends. He was trying to run into the burning house.

Frankie grabbed him around the neck as the other two dragged him away by his feet.

Within ten minutes, the fire department was attempting without much success to save the house. Saunders and Donnelly managed to get there quickly and were helping to restrain Taylor.

At dinner, Dick's phone rang. It showed Saunders was the caller. "The beach house is on fire. Taylor started it. Frankie and his friends caught him. Care to join us?"

Indeed, they did. All of them along with the police and fire department watched the fire consume the 100-year old house.

Back then, there were no fire codes, no demands for building with certain materials, and no way to really stop a fire once it hit the frame of the old house.

It wasn't long before the media showed up, taking photos, asking for comments.

Since the house belonged to Lily, they asked her how she felt about losing it. "Good. **THAT** Beach House was more like a **Murder** House." With that she turned and walked away holding Jake's hand.

Dora watched them holding on to each other. She realized this visit had had quite an impact on her son.

***

The next day at brunch, Dora put her arm around Lily. "You know, darling, the property is still worth a fortune?"

"I do. I don't want it. It's built on stolen money and murder." Lily was adamant and apparently strong willed.

"If you like, Dick and I do have a thought? The money could go to the Elder Abuse Task Force. Judge Wilson will make sure it goes to good use."

And with that, our Senior Sleuths, Dick and Dora, helped change the lives of many elderly people on the east end of Long Island.

And maybe even elsewhere.

Chapter Forty-Three
What are Friends For?

I t wasn't exactly a celebration.

It was more about closure.

There was certainly a sense of relief.

The friends gathered around a large round table in the Inn's dining room where the ocean was in view out the huge glass windows and they could hear the waves rolling on to the shore nearby.

Everyone needed to remove themselves, one way or another, from the ugly events that had unfolded here the past couple of weeks.

Lily and Jake sat next to each other, as did Cloud and Zero.

Frankie Socks and friends, as always, were elsewhere. Location unknown.

Chief Saunders and Detective Donnelly joined them as did Calvin Osborne, Dick's poker playing buddy, and Carson Gladstone, the newspaper reporter who wrote the stories for the New York City.

Carson loved to tease Dick. "Remember my mother Bertie is madly in love with you. I was going to bring her with me, but she's turned ninety and prefers to stay in Manhattan. She awaits your return with much anticipation. I expect you to be a gentleman."

Dora reached over and took her husband's hand with loving affection and smiled.

Dick nodded, appreciating his humor, grateful for the stories he wrote about the seriousness and "widespread epidemic" of elder abuse.

Both he and Osborne also wrote in-depth stories about THE MURDER HOUSE. They then followed up with expanded feature stories regarding the elderly abuse problem, its causes and terrible effects on the elderly population from one end of the country to the other and agreeing the root cause of elder abuse was almost always greed and money.

But it was not the only cause. Sometimes anger and revenge seemed to add a voice to this issue.

Talk at lunch included discussing human behavior and how arrogance and entitlement become motivating reasons and forces for that type of greed and criminal behavior.

As coffee was served and some left for work, the others knew it was time.

They were ready for new experiences and possibilities.

Jake, with his arm around Lily announced, "We are grateful to all of you, especially my parents. Lily and I are off to Paris."

Dick leaned over to Dora and whispered, "We are quite blessed, aren't we, dear?"

***

They certainly were.

So far none of the bad guys they met up with had managed to kill them.

Not yet anyhow.

Everyone had a plan for when they left the Hamptons.

***

We all do know, the best laid plans of mice and men often go awry (to quote Robert Burns from "To A Mouse"). Especially when Dick and Dora and their fearless cronies are involved.

Chapter Forty-Four
It's Time!

J ake and Lily left for Paris.

Dora wondered if they had marriage in their plans. She didn't dare ask, even though she desperately wanted to.

It was Paris and it seemed as if romance was everywhere there.

Lovers would find and feel it in charming cafes, walking along the streets and bridges over the Seine as tourists waved from river tours and cruises, as they visited museums filled with breathtaking art and from listening to French music encouraging the beauty of love in the city of lights. Even if one couldn't speak French, its language and music seemed to convey its meaning.

Lily and Jake certainly discovered a surprising sense of connection in their collective efforts as they helped fight off those who wanted to harm her, murdered her aunt and uncle and tried to deny her rights as their heir.

"At least some good will come from the sale of **THAT** Beach House." Lily looked relaxed as the waiter brought them another glass of wine.

Jake raised his glass. "To getting rid of the house, to gratitude for our family and friends and to our going to Paris." Others would leave for different destinations.

It was time for them too, for different reasons and different desires.

Zero and Cloud were going back to New Mexico.

Dick wondered if they would get married for real.

Zero glared at him and refused to answer when he had asked. The real issue was complicated. Could Cloud's family really accept him as her husband? Their culture and their heritage were so different.

Dora noticed Cloud seemed nervous and concerned about something happening with her family. Yet, Cloud dismissed any talk of it. Only saying, "It's nothing about Zero and me."

New Mexico is a mixed world of Native Americans, Hispanics and Anglos. Most had learned to live in harmony, yet there were those who held on to old angers and resentments. There were people who continued to behave with egregious acts of violence causing harm and spreading hatred.

Of course, there were other places, all too many, where that also existed. And people who enjoyed perpetuating such behaviors for their own gain.

Dora was deeply concerned, sensing a difference in Cloud's mood. "Cloud, call me anytime you want. Anytime!" Dora hugged her friend, knowing for her and Dick it was also time.

Dick and Dora Zimmerman were headed home. Frankie Socks would drive them to their Skyline Vista Condo in Manhattan and then head to his own apartment in the meatpacking district.

Frankie Socks had only returned to Manhattan a few years earlier after nearly twenty years away in the Witness Protection Program. As for the Zimms, as they were known by their city friends, they had spent a lifetime there. They had careers in the legal system and then retired to enjoy what they had created.

Okay, it turns out they didn't exactly retire.

True, Dick enjoyed playing poker with his buddies and occasional trips to the racetrack.

Dora was involved in different organizations, usually meant to save some piece of the planet or people suffering and struggling. Dick would too when Dora dragged him into one of her causes.

More often she dragged him into dealing with murder and mayhem.

Dinners out at the bar next door to the Skyline Vista Condos were enjoyed at least a couple times a week. The owner and his brother Detective Donnelly were good friends and they too were somehow dragged into Dora's penchant for fighting for justice.

When Zero was in the city he too joined them. He had also lived in the Skyline Vista Condos, a few floors down from the Zimms. He never could refuse Dora who he would call at times Lady D.

Good ole Zero, one resident described him. "You can always count on him sporting some outrageous fashion one is most likely never to forget. Gives us a reason to smile."

There was much more waiting for Dick and Dora, our senior sleuths as some called them, as they headed home. It was late spring and the tulips would be in full blossom on Park Avenue, people would have shed their heavy winter coats, Central Park would be filled with activities along with visitors riding through it in horse drawn carriages.

Manhattan store windows from Fifth Avenue to Madison Avenue, from the Village and SOHO, to the Upper West Side and Upper East Side were filled with spring and summer high fashions and high prices. The theatre district was active with tourists descending on the city as it warmed up and the restaurants literally were springing open their outdoor cafes. Few cared about the noise or traffic. At least most New Yorkers didn't. It was all part of city life and its endless energy.

And so as they headed back home, Dick and Dora sat back and smiled. As Frankie Socks paid the toll and drove through the Midtown Tunnel from Long Island to Manhattan, Dora leaned over and gave her husband a kiss on the cheek and took his hand.

"Who needs Paris," she whispered.

The Empire State building lit up seemed to welcom them as it did thousands of visitors each year.

Dora suddenly very still, realized, their time home might well be short. Her instincts after years as a judge rolled over her. "Cloud and Zero, something isn't right."

Anyone who knew Dick and Dora were aware of their propensity for getting involved in murders. It seemed they couldn't help themselves. Well, Dick might have ignored them, but not while he had Dora convincing him they needed to get involved in one murderous adventure after another.

"I have to protect Dora, you know?" he once told his poker buddies.

They all laughed. Zero had commented, "Come-on, without her your life would be a bore."

Dick smiled. "Without her my life would have no meaning."

End Notes: Elder Abuse and Neglect*

How many older Americans are abused? According to the National Council on Aging: Approximately 1 in 10 Americans aged 60+ have experienced some form of elder abuse. Some estimates range as high as 5 million elders are abused each year. One study estimated that only 1 in 14 cases of abuse are reported to authorities.

What is elder abuse and neglect?

Elder abuse includes physical, emotional, or sexual harm inflicted upon an older adult, their financial exploitation, or neglect of their welfare by people who are directly responsible for their care. In the U.S. alone, more than half a million reports of elder abuse reach authorities every year, and millions more cases go unreported.

As older adults become more physically frail, they're less able to take care of themselves, stand up to bullying, or fight back if attacked. Mental or physical ailments can make them more trying companions for those who live with them. And they may not see or hear as well or think as clearly as they used to, leaving openings for unscrupulous people to take advantage of them.

Elder abuse tends to take place where the senior lives: where their abusers are often adult children, other family members such as grandchildren, or a spouse or partner. Elder abuse can also occur in institutional settings, especially long-term care facilities.

If you suspect that an elderly person is at risk from a neglectful or overwhelmed caregiver, or being preyed upon financially, it's important to speak up. Everyone deserves to live in safety, with dignity and respect. These guidelines can help you recognize the warning signs of elder abuse, understand what the risk factors are, and learn how to prevent and report the problem.

Reporting elder abuse

If you are an elder who is being abused, neglected, or exploited, tell at least one person. Tell your doctor, a friend, or a family member whom you trust. Or call one of the helplines listed below. If you see an older adult being abused or neglected, don't hesitate to report the situation. And if you see future incidences of abuse, continue to call and report them. Each elder abuse report is a snapshot of what is taking place. The more information that you can provide, the better the chance the elder has of getting the quality of care they need. Older adults can become increasingly isolated from society and, with no work to attend, it can be easy for abuse cases to go unnoticed for long periods.

Many seniors don't report the abuse they face even if they're able. Some fear retaliation from the abuser, while others view having an abusive caretaker as better than having no caretaker and being forced to move out of their own home. When the caregivers are their children, they may feel ashamed that their children are inflicting harm or blame themselves. "If I'd been a better parent when they were younger, this wouldn't be happening." Or they just may not want children they love to get into trouble with the law. In any situation of elder abuse, it can be a real challenge to respect an older adult's right to autonomy while at the same time making sure they are properly cared for.

*https://www.helpguide.org > articles > abuse > elder-abuse-and-neglect

Author's Epilogue

A BOLD THIRD ACT
The Senior Sleuths Mysteries
by
M. Glenda Rosen (*aka* Marcia G. Rosen)

NO! I do not want to retire because I'm a senior. Absolutely not!

More than ever, seniors are living full and engaging lives. More than 45 million Americans are over the age of 65 and millions of them still work— some by choice, some by necessity.

In what I consider my BOLD THIRD ACT, I'm writing mysteries. I'm bringing my passion for writing together with my rather unusual upbringing. In doing so, I am writing with more insight and purpose. As seniors, we can use our life experiences—whether failures, challenges or successes—to bring about enjoyable and productive lives filled with doing something we relate to and love. This is why the seniors in the mysteries I write are strong, smart and active main characters. They love and are great at figuring out the puzzles of people's behavior, including murder!

Mysteries and crime are probably in my DNA. The environment I grew up in seemed perfectly natural to me. It's what I saw everyday: My father was a bookie. He also owned a gambling hall where the men played pool in the front and poker in a private back room. My father and his partners would count the take from sports bets at our kitchen table. Once there was a raid on his partner's apartment, which was right across from ours!

My father's close friends had names like The Gig, Gimp and Doc. So, it makes sense that I'm fascinated by slightly shady characters, crime and mystery stories. Once, I wrote a memoir and referred to my mother as my father's "gun moll." Believe me, she was a character as well!

I've been a business owner for more than 40 years, which includes having a successful marketing and public relations agency for more than 20 years. I used to explain to clients that I was a "business detective," finding solutions to problems that seemed a mystery to them. Of course, people and life in general are often a mystery.

My kids have encouraged me to "Go for it!" They do not want me to slow down, sit around and dream of days past. They don't want me to use going to doctors as a social outlet as so many elderly people do. They don't even want me to have grey hair!

To those who do not agree: Sorry! I think I still have much to offer and enjoy. Positive aging is important to me, and writing is my way of showing it.

I used to tell friends that I was too old to see my dreams and ambitions to be a successful author come true. Yet, I refused to give up trying, and now my new mystery series "The Senior Sleuths" is being published and more are on the way with my publisher, Level Best Books.

I'd often ask business and professional women: "What voices in your head do you need to eliminate? Get rid of the negative voices that say, 'Who do you think you are?' and 'You can't do it.'"

Now in my senior life, I'm reminded through conversations over a cup of coffee with my friends, some my age and some younger, "We all matter." What you want and who you are matters.

We can make a difference at any age. Moreover, as we grow older, we can also share our experience, knowledge and, even at times, a good bit of wisdom.

In my mystery series, "The Senior Sleuths," my senior characters represent my beliefs with energy and enthusiasm. These characters are my voice and reflect my truths."

Marcia Glenda Rosen

Dead in A Storm

The Senior Sleuths (Book 4)
Dick and Dora Zimmerman…With Zero…The Bookie

by

M. Glenda Rosen

Prologue
Disturbances

All storms cause a disturbance

Nature's storms disturb our home and our safety.

Storms of protest demands can affect our consciousness of right and wrong.

Emotional storms provoked by secrets and lies, or, by anger, rage and abuse, disturb our well-being.

They disturb our sanity and our souls.

A storm can happen with little or no warning...

...or, build up until they explode with an intense violence causing serious damage.

Zero had left a one-word message for his friends, "Help."

Two days later, Dick and Dora Zimmerman landed in the Albuquerque International Airport near midnight. The bright lights spanning across the city below proved a false promise. Complete darkness would have been more fitting.

Dick and Dora would discover there was a threatening storm ultimately ending in murder.

It had begun with an unsigned note mailed to Cloud, the woman Zero married not once but twice, "For The Love of Revenge"

The storm had given frightening warnings.

Dick and Dora Face Murder and Mayhem in A Modern Noir Style as Soft-Boiled Sleuths

Acknowledgements

How fortunate I am to have many energetic and accomplished seniors as friends and fellow travelers. We support and often guide each other through the strange and at times unsettling world of being a senior.

As always my heartfelt thanks to my publisher Level Best Books who is providing my senior life with great joy.

With gratitude for, and memory of, my dear friend and ardent supporter Joyce Olcese.

Author Photo credit: Peter Hemming.

About the Author

Marcia Rosen (*aka* M.Glenda Rosen) is author of ten books including *The Senior Sleuths* and *Dying To Be Beautiful Mystery Series*, and *The Gourmet Gangster, Mysteries and Menus* (with her son Jory Rosen), published by Level Best Books. Marcia is also author of *The Woman's Business Therapist* and award-winning *My Memoir Workbook*. She was owner of a successful national marketing and public relations agency in New Mexico and New York, and has worked with many author clients. To that end she has given classes and workshops and has guest lectured on topics such as *Encouraging the Writer Within You, Getting Published, Now What? (Book Marketing), Writing Mysteries...Not A Mystery, Writing From Your Soul,* and

The Gangster's Daughter. She has published numerous articles and is a member of Sisters In Crime Los Angeles and Albuquerque, Central Coast Writers, Public Safety Writer's Association, and Rocky Mountain Fiction Writers.

www.theseniorsleuths.com   and
www.creativebookconcept.com

Also by M. Glenda Rosen

The Gourmet Gangster, Mysteries and Menus by The Family
The Senior Sleuths Mysteries: Dead In Seat 4-A
The Senior Sleuths Mysteries: Dead In Bed
The Senior Sleuths Mysteries: Dead In THAT Beach House (2020)
The Senior Sleuths Mysteries: Dead In A Storm (2021
***
Dying To Be Beautiful: Without A Head
Dying To Be Beautiful: Fashion Queen
Dying To Be Beautiful: Fake Beauty
Dying To Be Beautiful: Fat Free
***
My Memoir Workbook
The Woman's Business Therapist: Eliminate the MindBlocks & RoadBlocks to Success

And...

Co-authored a series of "Do-It-Write Booklets" sponsored by New York City bank and materials on "How to Market Your Practice" for a national pharmaceutical company. Executive Editor of Single Scene Magazine (while married).

Marcia lives in Carmel, California, and has author clients in New York City, Atlanta, Albuquerque, Long Island, the Hamptons, and Vancouver.

CPSIA information can be obtained
at www.ICGtesting.com
Printed in the USA
FSHW011258280820
73313FS